LAST CHANCE

As we run into the dugout, none of us has any doubt that without a miracle, the Coyotes were going to cream us again.

We get no miracle. Instead, we get three quick at-bats and three quick outs. At least we were hitting the ball, I thought—nobody struck out—but the hits were not falling in.

As we grabbed our gloves to take the field, Frankie tells my dad something we can all hear. "Let me pitch," he says. "I can do it."

We freeze. If anyone else had suggested the idea, we would've all sneered. It was outside the realm of reality. Beyond belief. A guy on the mound with his arm in a sling? But the reality was, we were ready to believe in something better than the reality we faced. Dad was too.

If he could increase our chances—even to the tiniest degree—of beating Cartridge for the league championship, Dad would've listened to a drunken ump slumped against the dugout. So he tells Frankie, "Let's go to the mound and give you a little tryout."

OTHER BOOKS YOU MAY ENJOY

Baseball CRAZY

TEN STORIES THAT COVER ALL THE BASES

EDITED BY NANCY E. MERCADO

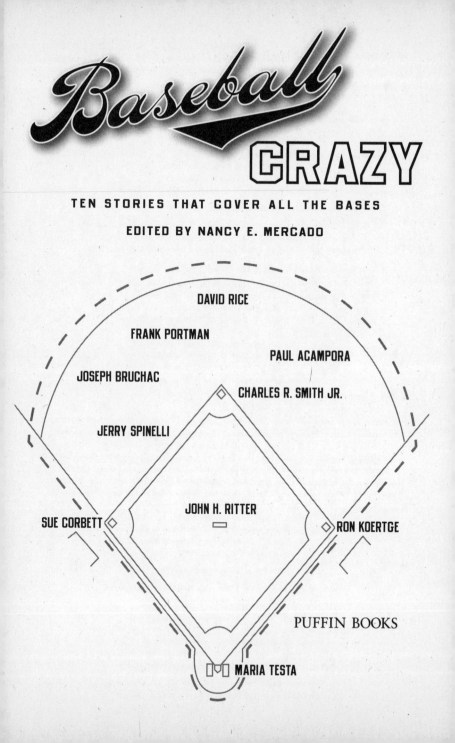

DAVID RICE

FRANK PORTMAN

PAUL ACAMPORA

JOSEPH BRUCHAC

CHARLES R. SMITH JR.

JERRY SPINELLI

JOHN H. RITTER

SUE CORBETT

RON KOERTGE

PUFFIN BOOKS

MARIA TESTA

PUFFIN BOOKS

Published by the Penguin Group

Penguin Young Readers Group, 345 Hudson Street, New York, New York 10014, U.S.A.

Penguin Group (Canada), 90 Eglinton Avenue East, Suite 700, Toronto, Ontario, Canada M4P 2Y3
(a division of Pearson Penguin Canada Inc.)

Penguin Books Ltd, 80 Strand, London WC2R 0RL, England

Penguin Ireland, 25 St Stephen's Green, Dublin 2, Ireland (a division of Penguin Books Ltd)

Penguin Group (Australia), 250 Camberwell Road, Camberwell, Victoria 3124, Australia
(a division of Pearson Australia Group Pty Ltd)

Penguin Books India Pvt Ltd, 11 Community Centre, Panchsheel Park, New Delhi - 110 017, India

Penguin Group (NZ), 67 Apollo Drive, Rosedale, North Shore 0632, New Zealand
(a division of Pearson New Zealand Ltd)

Penguin Books (South Africa) (Pty) Ltd, 24 Sturdee Avenue, Rosebank, Johannesburg 2196, South Africa

Registered Offices: Penguin Books Ltd, 80 Strand, London WC2R 0RL, England

First published in the United States of America by Dial Books for Young Readers,
a division of Penguin Young Readers Group, 2008
Published by Puffin Books, a division of Penguin Young Readers Group, 2009

1 3 5 7 9 10 8 6 4 2

"The Great Gus Zernial and Me" © Jerry Spinelli, 2008
"Mark Pang and the Impossible Square" © Frank Portman, 2008
"Fall Ball" © Sue Corbett, 2008
"Great Moments in Baseball" © Paul Acampora, 2008
"Riding the Pine: A Play" © Ron Koertge, 2008
"Tomboy Forgiveness" © David Rice, 2008
"Smile Like Jeter" © Maria Testa, 2008
"Baseball Crazy" © John H. Ritter, 2008
"Just Like Grampy" © Charles R. Smith Jr., 2008
"Ball Hawk" © Joseph Bruchac, 2008
All rights reserved

THE LIBRARY OF CONGRESS HAS CATALOGED THE DIAL BOOKS FOR YOUNG READERS EDITION AS FOLLOWS:
Baseball crazy : ten short stories that cover all the bases / edited by Nancy E. Mercado.
p. cm.
Contents: The great Gus Zernial and me / by Jerry Spinelli—Mark Pang and the impossible
square / by Frank Portman—Fall ball / by Sue Corbett—Great moments in baseball / by Paul
Acampora—Riding the pine: a play / by Ron Koertge—Tomboy forgiveness / by David Rice—Smile
like Jeter / by Maria Testa—Baseball crazy / by John H. Ritter—Just like Grampy / by Charles R.
Smith Jr.—Ball hawk / by Joseph Bruchac.
ISBN: 978-0-8037-3162-2 (hc)
1. Baseball stories, American. 2. Children's stories, American.
[1. Baseball—Fiction. 2. Short stories.] I. Mercado, Nancy E., date.
PZ5.B314 2008 [Fic]—dc22 2007026649

Puffin Books ISBN 978-0-14-241371-5

Designed by Jasmin Rubero • Text set in New Century Schoolbook
Printed in the United States of America

LINEUP

COACH: _Nancy E. Mercado_   **TEAM:** _Baseball Crazy_

Introduction

I am surrounded by baseball fans. People who can quote the stats, know all the history, and who feel an itch to play when they walk by an empty ball field.

Me? I've always been more of a fair-weather fan, interested in baseball when it served me (like during a particularly dramatic World Series or when a boy I liked was interested), and to be honest, just seeing a baseball field in a photograph can bring back some painful and potent memories of grade-school humiliation.

But then . . . the stories for this collection came trickling in. And being in the company of ten more people who not only know their baseball, and love their baseball, but, best of all, can write stories that encapsulate the spectacular wonder, terror, and joy of baseball, made me feel differently.

I asked these authors to write stories that went beyond simply telling about the game itself and explored more the feelings and emotions we attach to playing, watching, and competing. And I'm not going to ruin the game by telling you the play-by-play of what happens in each story. But I will tell you that these ten narratives offer up a compelling panorama of the sport, from the perspective of kids who love the game and those who hate it, the view from the stands, from behind the plate and from the bench. There's even a story about softball thrown in there, proving that a softer ball certainly doesn't diminish the emotional intensity of a game against rivals.

So what happened to this fair-weather fan after editing these stories? The difference is subtle. These days I find myself lingering longer on the ESPN channel, following individual players' careers with a bit more interest, and even entertaining notions of re-joining the local softball league. Could it be that the stories have changed me? Well, I'll certainly never know batting averages, and I'll win the lottery before I ever hit a home run, but now I can truly understand the twinkle in someone's eye when talking about a recent game. People are just baseball crazy, that's all!

Best,

Nancy

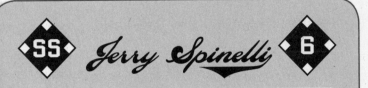

SS *Jerry Spinelli* **6**

POSITION: SHORTSTOP | *ROOKIE YEAR: 1982

*BBI: 27 (actually 31 if you count the first four unpublished ones)

CAREER HIGHLIGHTS: Oh boy—let's say this: It underlies everything else and is much harder to achieve than I ever knew in high school. I make my living writing stories.

FAVORITE TEAM: Philadelphia Phillies

FAVORITE PLAYER: Larry Bowa

BEST GAME EVER: The day I got two hits and two RBIs to lead the Norristown Brick Company to the Pennsylvania Knee-Hi baseball championship when I was fourteen.

THE GREAT GUS ZERNIAL AND ME

by Jerry Spinelli

"Look at you. You're dirty again. Your friend is here."

The nun hauled me to the nearest sink and scrubbed my face nearly raw. She took scant care to keep the soap out of my eyes. It was strictly from the soap that I cried. The rough treatment I was used to. I expected it. I deserved it.

I lived in an orphanage. I was therefore known as a "homie." That alone was enough to make me feel different, but even among the homies I seemed to be an outcast.

For one thing, I was a wet-the-bed, a designation that entitled me to be paddled every night as I emerged dripping wet from the shower. After lights out I would stay awake as long as I could, only to be betrayed by sleep. In the morning, with the inevitability of eternal judgment, I would waken to the faint damp mustiness of my sin.

For another thing, I was smart. I could already read in the first grade. My hand was forever waving wildly in the classroom. Sometimes a whole day seemed to pass with no one volunteering answers but me. Time and again the nun would scan the seats in vain for another hand. She would try to coax answers from slumping heads. Then, with an audible sigh, she would finally turn to me and flicking her forefinger release me from my bondage of silence. Though my answers were invariably correct, the nun never seemed as happy to receive them as I did to give them.

Then one day during recess in the playground, three of the bigger (and dumber) kids in class came up to me. As usual I was in the dirt near the roots of a huge old tree, playing marbles against myself. One of the big kids said, "Stand up."

I stood up.

"How come you always raise yer hand?" he said.

I shrugged.

"How come?"

"I know the answers."

"Well, don't raise yer hand no more."

I squealed, "What!"

"You deef?" he snarled. Then he placed my biggest

marble on top of my shoe, and with the heel of his shoe he ground the marble into my foot.

I was too upset to appreciate the befuddled look on the nun's face the rest of the day as she kept glancing at my firmly desk-bound hand.

Then there was the great three-day mystery. It took place in the classroom. On the first day it started with the nun turning from the blackboard and sniffing into the space above our heads, rabbit-like. Her chalk hand was still pasted on the board, stopped in the middle of a word. Several more times she sniffed that day, and once, while we were doing our spelling, bent over and ran her pointer along the black dusty space beneath the radiator.

On the second day she turned from the blackboard, chalk hand and all, and announced, "All right—out. Out!" We filed outside, the head nun went in, and a half hour later we returned. All windows were open, as was the door.

On the third day she came stalking down the aisles. My eyes were fixed on my spelling, but I could trace her movement by the soft rustle of her skirt. It stopped right behind me. Then came the most horrible shriek: "Eeeeeey ahhhh-HAH!"

It was me. It seems I had an unconscious habit of slipping out of my shoes while sitting in class. And it seems, as I was to learn later, that I was afflicted with a condition in which a perspiring foot, however otherwise clean, gives off an undue degree of odor.

Of course, I was thenceforth forbidden to go any-where unshod outside the shower room. And kids I never knew found it impossible to pass me without pinching their nostrils. "Feet," they would honk.

These things made me feel I was the fly in every pie. Apparently I had been born with a terrible power: I spoiled everything around me.

I had forgotten that a friend would be coming for me on this particular Saturday. (*Friend* was the Home's word for anyone who came to visit you or take you out. A friend was usually a perfect stranger, but could also be a relative or even a long-lost parent. Some of the homies had a long string of friends. This was to be my first.) Why a friend would want to visit me I couldn't imagine.

He was a fat little man, shorter than the nuns. He held a straw hat in front of himself with both hands.

He smiled. "How would you like to go to a ball game?"

"Okay," I said.

It turned out to be a baseball game in the city. It might as well have been Rumanian rugby. I had heard of baseball but I had never played it and knew next to nothing about it. Except for marbles I was woefully unathletic.

The game was at Shibe Park. A sign said "Home of the Philadelphia A's." *Home.* Now it began to make sense: The A's were orphans too. They were playing the Boston Red Sox. The man (Mr. Coleman was his name) took me by the hand, stunned and docile, through dusty, echo-y, mustard-sweet tunnels, up endless iron stairways, finally to emerge onto what I was told were the bleachers. We were beyond what was known as left field.

It was the most beautiful sight I had ever seen— a vast fan-shaped emerald-green lawn. I had never known the earth could be so immaculate. It was all so ordered, so perfect. Two utterly straight and pure white lines diverged from a point called home plate and created the borders of this perfection along with the tall green fence that they intersected. I was vaguely comforted that the white lines did not diverge forever.

Men toting rakes and other implements came out of nowhere and swarmed over the field.

Mr. Coleman saw my puzzlement and chuckled. "That's not baseball. That's the grounds crew. Watch the tractor."

And sure enough a little blue tractor came putting out from under the grandstand, dragging behind what looked like a large window screen. It headed for the tawny, half-moon-shaped portion of the field, where no grass grew. From first base to third base it traveled, tracing exquisite loops, and what the screen passed over it left in a condition so smooth and flat and unmarked that it could not possibly be called dirt.

Meanwhile the men with rakes were smoothing the field around the bases where the tractor screen could not reach. And other men were smoothing out the pitcher's mound and the home plate area, or painting the home plate itself, or repairing the white lines where someone had stepped on them.

Then, as if by signal, the men began leaving the field. The rakers trailed their rakes behind, so as to erase their own footprints.

"Now the water," said Mr. Coleman.

Two men were wheeling a large hose reel out near the pitcher's mound. They pulled out two hoses and began to spray the dirt portion.

"Keeps the dust down," said Mr. Coleman, answering my unspoken question.

Dust or no dust, I did not like the water men. I found myself urging them to pass over the dirt lightly, but they insisted on wetting it down so thoroughly that in a few minutes the infield had turned from yellowish to dark gray.

There was a lilt of expectancy in Mr. Coleman's next announcement, and an almost conspiratorial whisper: "Now—the bases."

What's wrong with the bases, I wondered, noting the three gray squares on the infield. Then to my amazement I discovered I had not been looking at the real bases at all. They were just covers, jackets, which a man was removing. Now the true bases were revealed—

sparkling Chiclet-white cubes that had never been touched. And I saw now the real reason they had made the infield so dark with water—so as to dramatically set off the gleaming bases.

The base man left the field. And there it was, more beautiful, more perfect than when I had entered. The grounds crew, before our very eyes, had done as much a miracle as man could do.

I leaped to my feet. I clapped and cheered. What a performance!

A few seconds later I was crushed. Men in baggy flannel knickers were springing onto the field, scattering to all points. I felt on my own skin every footprint they left on the immaculate infield.

Until that moment Mr. Coleman had been a man of smiles. Now he was out-and-out laughing, his eyes watering. "These are the players," he said, nodding toward the field. I felt his hand cup my shoulder and pull me a little toward him.

"Now the game's ready to start."

Then he drew his face near to mine and whispered, "See him?" He was pointing to a player jogging across the grass toward us. He didn't stop till he was almost to the fence. Then he turned around and faced home plate. He simply stood there. He was almost directly beneath us, so there wasn't much to see except his blue cap and his shoulders and a large blue number on his back. "That's Gus Zernial," Mr. Coleman told me.

"Who's he?" I said.

"The left fielder."

"What's he doing?""

"He's playing left field."

"He's just standing there."

"Well, that's right. He doesn't have much to do out here. But wait'll he gets to bat." Here Mr. Coleman put his lips right to my ear. "Maybe he'll hit a home run."

I turned to him full face. "Is that good?"

Mr. Coleman said nothing. He simply closed his eyes and smiled and nodded profoundly, and I knew that a home run, whatever it was, was a very, very good thing.

The game as I recall it was a series of whispered prophecies come true, few of them having to do with the actual action of the game.

Mr. Coleman told me to keep an eye on the third-base coach. And for inning after inning the third-base coach kept me enthralled with his antics and contortions and twitches. He seemed plagued by either poison ivy or a particularly insistent mosquito. Even the batters seemed distracted, for they kept turning away from the pitcher to look at the third-base coach.

"He's giving the signs," said Mr. Coleman.

"Oh," I said.

When the hot dog man came down our aisle Mr. Coleman raised his arm and shouted, "Two!" Then, as he leaned across me to pass along the money: "Watch the mustard. Watch."

I watched. Like that of the grounds crew it was a virtuoso performance. Two hot dog rolls in the same hand—up goes the lid of the white carton and into the rising steam with gleaming silver tweezers—a slight hesitation (he's fishing for the best!)—then they're out, two reddish dripping morsels—deftly laid in their rolls. *"Waaatch . . ."* came my last warning. Into the giant mustard jar with a tongue depressor and . . . and . . . it was done. Before my eyes could digest the sight, the hot dogs were being passed down the row to us. All I had seen was a lightning flicker of the tongue depressor over the rolls, and yet when they reached us, sure enough, anointing each hot dog was a neat strip of creamy bright yellow mustard.

Even as I chewed, my eyes never left the lightning-handed hot dog man until he disappeared into the crowd.

A player slid. Home plate vanished under a layer of dust. Mr. Coleman nudged me. "Watch the umpire." The umpire pulled something from his hip pocket—it was a little whisk broom. With brisk, assured ceremony he squatted in the dust and—whish-whish-whish—home plate reappeared. I decided then and there I wanted to be an umpire.

There were many other prophecies. That everyone would boo at such and such a time. That the manager would spit every time he left the dugout. That when the manager and umpire argued they would touch noses. That it would become very hot in the bleachers. That in the seventh inning everyone in the ball park would stand up and stretch.

And they all came true, every one. I relished the predictability of it all. My favorite was the seventh inning stretch. "Now?" I kept asking. "Now," he finally said. I shot up, determined to be first. I looked around. Slowly they were rising, all around me, by the thousands, rising for the seventh inning stretch. Not a single soul was left sitting. I did not honestly feel stiff or tired, but I'm sure no one could tell by the great, long stretch that I did.

Inning after inning Gus Zernial trotted back and forth from left field to the dugout.

"Did he hit a home run yet?" I kept pestering.

"Not yet," said Mr. Coleman. The confident glee was gone from his voice. He sounded a little like a priest. "It's not for sure, now. All he can do is try. Don't get your hopes up too high."

I guess my hopes were up too high, for Mr. Coleman stared worriedly at me for a minute. The smile returned. "But I'll tell you one thing," he whispered. "If he *does* hit a home run, do you know what he'll do?"

"What?"

"He'll tip his cap."

"He will?"

He placed his hand over his heart. "Promise."

It was in the last inning of the ball game when a sudden commotion erupted around me. Everyone in the bleachers seemed to shout in unison and bolt to their feet, including Mr. Coleman. Then I saw it—the baseball—dove-white, like the bases, falling from the sun-squinting sky, angel-white against the murky girded ceiling, engulfed at last into a mass of frantically straining arms several aisles away.

I didn't have to be told. It was a home run.

"Gus Zernial?" I screamed up at Mr. Coleman. "Gus Zernial?"

The way he hugged me, I knew it was.

What a wonderful thing is a home run, I thought. The joy that it brought. The ecstasy. I could only think of it as a gift, a kind of salvation. It was a religious thing, a home run, something sacramental. I thought of the priest offering the wafer, and of the Magi bearing gifts, and of the archbishop who came every Christmas and we knew then that we would get ice cream. Now there was the home run, delivered unto the bleachers. Now there was the priest and there were the Magi and there was the archbishop and there was Gus Zernial.

I shaded my eyes so as to most clearly see the man trotting around the bases. I saw him touch every bag. I saw him shake the hand of the third-base coach as he passed by. I saw him step decisively upon home plate and shake the hands of the next batter and the bat boy, and I saw him received into the welcoming arms of the dugout. But I did not see him tip his cap.

I kept silent, not wanting to show disappointment. All of Mr. Coleman's other prophecies had come true, even the "not for sure" home run. Who was I to quibble over one unfulfilled detail? I—a wiseacre wet-the-bed stinky-footed homie.

But inside me I couldn't help quibbling. Something was longing for the tipped cap even more than for the home run. Without the tipped cap the home run was incomplete, tradition was left dangling. I couldn't help wondering: *Is it me? Does Gus Zernial know I'm in the bleachers?* I tightened my shoelaces.

The answer came a few minutes later. Gus Zernial was trotting out to take his place in left field, and again the bleachers erupted. They flailed their arms. They screamed and whistled. "Gus! Gus! Gus!" they chanted.

But Gus Zernial did not seem to hear. He merely stood there facing the infield, while just behind and above him five thousand people were going mad.

I dared not join the crowd. Oh, I wanted to. I wanted to chant his name and cheer him. I wanted to go mad too. But I was afraid he might see me.

Suddenly the cheering shot to a deafening pitch. Down below Gus Zernial was turning—not all the way, just his head and shoulders, so that the brim of the blue cap was now facing the bleachers and you could see the fancy white A on it, and now his head was tilting upward and there was the face of the great Gus Zernial and he was looking right up into the bleachers—*he was looking right at me*—and with a delicacy I would never expect he took the blue brim between his thumb and forefinger and briefly, briefly and forever, tipped his cap.

SF *Frank Portman* **10**

POSITION: SHORT FIELD | *ROOKIE YEAR: 2006

*BBI: 2

CAREER HIGHLIGHTS: I believe I still hold the all-time record for most times hit with a pitch in a single season in the Lions League.

FAVORITE TEAM: San Francisco Seals

FAVORITE PLAYER: Lefty O'Doul
vs. Gary Kasparov

BEST GAME EVER: Fischer / Spassky
Reykjavik 1972, Game 2.

MARK PANG AND THE IMPOSSIBLE SQUARE

by Frank Portman

Just like in a movie, someone hit an unexpected pop-up to right center, directly toward Mark Pang, and everybody groaned.

No one expected Mark Pang to catch that ball. Of course they didn't. The coach had one instruction for Mark Pang when it came to fielding, and the kids on the team agreed: If the ball ever comes anywhere near you, just get away from it and let someone else handle the situation.

Mark Pang could see their point. There had been maybe a couple of times during the early season when he had somehow managed to pick up a ground ball, and both times, instead of throwing it to an infielder like he was supposed to, he froze. He couldn't handle people staring at him, yelling at him. It made him nervous. Then it was like his brain short-circuited. And the longer he remained frozen, the more they yelled; and the more they yelled, the more frozen he felt, like he was a statue or something. It almost seemed like it could go on forever, a permanently angry crowd screaming till the end of time at a statue of an eleven-year-old with a terrified expression and a ball in his outstretched hand. As long as they kept yelling, the statue would remain, a monument to how Mark Pang totally sucked at baseball. Schools could arrange field trips so students could study it, the most unusual statue in the greater Bay Area.

"Don't be a hotshot out there," was how the coach put it. What that meant was: We'll let you wear a uniform and stand in the outfield every now and then, as long as you don't interfere with our game. Mark Pang usually had little trouble holding up his end of the bargain. But this particular ball was looking like a deal-breaker, speeding directly toward him, somewhere between a pop-up and a line drive, which might otherwise be seen as an easy out, but which because Mark Pang was involved looked like a hit. The aluminum bat clattered to the ground, and the batter was already nearly halfway to first base, whooping—or Mark Pang imagined he was the one who was whooping. In the stands, the parents of the Dark Blue team, Hillmont Stationers, were screaming with joy; the parents of the

Green team, Pete's Old-Fashion Italian Delicatessen, were screaming with rage. But everybody was screaming, and for the same reason: Mark Pang.

The saying about right field is that you're out there watching the dandelions grow, meaning that the right fielder usually never has to do much of anything and is more or less alone with his thoughts. Mark Pang wasn't the right fielder, not quite, though the idea was the same. In Mark Pang's league, they had changed the rules to make it so that all kids could participate, regardless of ability. There were no tryouts; if your dad signed you up and paid the fee, you were on the team. Everyone had an equal chance at bat, and everyone had a chance on the field as well. That's the only way guys like Mark Pang end up on baseball teams at all. Why guys who were good at baseball would want to be in this league was kind of puzzling. Mark Pang had never been able to figure it out. Some of them were in "real" leagues too, so maybe they saw this as their fun, kick-back, goof-off league.

In order to make it easier to put the entire team on the field in every game, and to ensure that the sucky players like Mark Pang would do a bit less damage, they had created two additional outfield positions, kind of like two outfield shortstops: left short center and right short center. Mark Pang was playing right short center, a position with even less action and responsibility than actual right field, if such a thing could be imagined.

Nevertheless, Mark Pang was always too worried to watch dandelions. Because there was a weakness in the coach's Keep Mark Pang Away from the Ball at All Costs strategy, even with five outfielders. It had to do with math, or maybe it was more like geometry.

Imagine the outfield as a grid made of Mark Pang–sized squares, with Mark Pang in a "ready position" in one of them. The player in this Mark Pang square, that is, Mark Pang, would control this square, plus the surrounding eight squares and perhaps an additional square on each horizontal and diagonal line extending from the center, for a total of seventeen squares. If Mark Pang moved to another square, his entire group of seventeen squares, his zone of control, moved with him. From the crack of the bat to the landing of the ball, there was just enough time to move three, maybe four squares in any direction. So if Mark Pang "looked alive" when the ball came his way, he could move his zone of control up to four squares out of the way so as not to interfere, while another, better player would move into position to catch and field the ball that Mark Pang would most likely have missed.

However, and this was a little known but mathematically certain fact, there was always at least one impossible square. That is, there was one square where it was not mathematically possible for Mark Pang to move farther away from the ball than any of the other players who were moving toward it. Ordinarily, the likelihood of the ball being caught and fielded was greater the farther away Mark Pang was from it. But it was different in the impossible square: There, it was Mark Pang or nothing. It was an extremely rare situation, but it happened. So instead of watching dandelions, Mark Pang spent his fielded innings praying: "Not the impossible square, please, God, not the impossible square." Usually it worked. But not this time. It was horrifying, but true: In this particular game, in this particular inning, with this particular ball, Mark Pang was in the middle of a developing impossible-square situation.

The ball was speeding toward him. Mark Pang knew he had to tune out the screaming from the stands, the groaning from the field. He tried not to think about his father near the dugout, and the pained, embarrassed expression that was certain to be on his face. He tried to keep his eye on the ball, even as he felt himself freezing up; by Mark Pang's calculations, he only had about three-quarters of a second before it would be too late to take action.

Mark Pang did some of his best thinking standing in right short center. He certainly had had a lot of time to develop his ideas about zones of control and the spatial relationships between outfielders and their squares. Mark Pang was a bit better at chess than baseball, though he thought he understood both games pretty well. He could see similarities between the two, that's for sure. But in chess, you never had to worry about any of the pieces screwing up, or getting nervous or self-conscious. When there's an impossible square in a chess game, it's solely because of the positions of the pieces in relation to one another, not because a bishop freezes up or a rook doesn't show enough "hustle."

"Hustle" was a problem for Mark Pang. He was— well, his mom would say "heavyset," to be polite. A bit overweight. Not too bad, really. There were fatter guys around than Mark Pang. But people, even those who were basically nice and meant no harm, would find it funny when Mark Pang ran. They couldn't help it. And the mean ones would sometimes make this "boing-boing" sound whenever they saw Mark Pang hurrying anywhere, not just in the outfield toward an impossible square, but at school or on the street. If he ran during lunch period, there would always be someone who would make a cafeteria-oriented joke, like: "Quick! Before all the food runs out!" They couldn't help it. Running looked worst when your arms were flailing, so you had to be careful to keep them loosely crooked and down at your sides (though not too far down at your sides—that looked even weirder). An easy, unhurried, confident trot was best, if you could pull it off, but it's actually a lot harder than it sounds.

So running without looking weird was tough any way you sliced it. But in this Impossible-Square Situation, it was even worse, because you pretty much had to be facing the oncoming ball if you wanted to stand a chance of actually catching it. That meant you had to attempt to trot not only unhurriedly and confidently, and not only with loosely crooked arms, but also *backwards,* and with enough "hustle" so that you would reach the impossible square at precisely the right moment. Mark Pang had seen this done many, many times, by pro ballplayers and even by fielders in his own league. When it's done right, it can be a thing of beauty, as his dad would say. But Mark Pang was somewhat less than confident in his running backwards skills. And if you think people find it funny when a fat kid runs down the hall toward the cafeteria, that's nothing compared to how funny they find it when a fat kid trips and falls on his butt.

Mark Pang didn't really have a choice, though. He started trotting backwards toward where he guessed the impossible square would end up being, even though the whole scenario had disaster written all over it. What else was he going to do?

Now, Mark Pang had this tendency, in his day-to-day life, of trying to relieve the pressure by clowning around. He didn't want it to look like he took things too seriously. He would make a funny face and shuffle behind a door, and then shuffle back out again except that he would be making a different funny face. Or he would just stare at people with a strange, frozen expression, and then say, after a pause of just the right length and with a somber tone: "Ding dong" or "Algebra lettuce." That kind of thing. People liked his off-the-wall humor, and he liked their liking it. So Mark Pang had this idea that it would be pretty funny if he smiled a broad, motionless smile as he was trotting backwards and, instead of stopping at the impossible square and attempting to catch the ball, he just continued to trot backwards, tipping his hat mechanically like a robot, letting the ball drop next to him, and proceeding smilingly backwards and at a steady pace to the edge of the outfield, then around the fence, then up the slope, then past the junior high and down the street and all the way to his house. No one, least of all Mark Pang himself, was expecting the ball to be caught anyway, so it wouldn't make a difference to the score.

But, of course, he couldn't *really* do that. Everyone would be furious. He would be off the team, and his dad would be disappointed and embarrassed and probably yell and demand an explanation of what the heck was the matter with him.

There was a third possibility, of course: He could just turn around and run as fast as he could without regard for how stupid he looked or how mad his dad would be, just get the hell out of there, throw his mitt in the Dumpster and never play baseball again. But Mark Pang knew he wouldn't do that either. No, what Mark Pang was going to do was to make for the impossible square and stand in it. Then he was going to hold up his mitt and place the other hand behind the thumb part and hope for the best, even though there was a near certainty that he would screw it up and that everyone would be reminded once again of how much they hated him and how they wished he was somebody else's kid, or on somebody else's team. He didn't really have a choice.

Mark Pang's dad was pretty gung-ho about baseball. It was a thinking game as well as a playing game, he said, which made it the world's greatest sport. Mark Pang agreed with all that, though sometimes he found himself wondering why it was supposed to be fun to play a game you weren't all that good at, a game that, let's face it, you probably weren't going to get that much better at no matter how long you stood in Right Short Center, no matter how many times you went to the batting cages. And how much fun could it be to be the dad of the team's worst player? If Mark Pang's dad had ever had any thoughts along those lines, he kept them well-hidden. He was very enthusiastic about the Green team and attended every game, saying things like "Good eye" if the umpire called a ball when Mark Pang was up, or "Good cut" when he swung and missed, or "Shake it off" if he was ever hit by a pitch, or "At ease" when—actually, Mark Pang wasn't all that sure what "At ease" was supposed to mean or refer to. His dad said it all the time, though. Sometimes it seemed like all Mark Pang's dad ever wanted to talk about was the Lions League standings. Mark Pang went along with it because he didn't want to disappoint him, and he never let on that he thought that was a little weird. Didn't he have more important things to worry about than the Green and the Dark Blue?

Mark Pang's mom was interested in Mark Pang's baseball career for health reasons, because she was worried about his weight. "It's good to get out in the sun," she would say, as if standing in the sun could perform some kind of slimming miracle. Mark Pang had the impression that his mom didn't quite realize just how accurate that description was: For a sport, baseball involved a lot of standing around, especially for a guy like Mark Pang. Even now, in the most active moment in Mark Pang's season so far, the mad dash for the impossible square would only involve trotting backwards for a distance of around five or six feet at the most. If she really wanted him to get exercise, she should have been encouraging him to run to the cafeteria every day rather than to continue being a member of a baseball team. That's, like, thirty times the distance.

The bigger you are, the more surface area you have, the more you sweat. And being nervous just makes it worse. Mark Pang was dripping, as though he had just gotten out of the shower. And of course the baseball uniform was no help. Way back, when they originally came up with the baseball uniform, they obviously hadn't been thinking about the possibility that a slightly overweight nervous kid like Mark Pang might have to run backwards six feet in the direction of an impossible square while wearing one on a hot day in the California sun while everyone was screaming at him. It was bulky and hot, and had several layers, which was bad enough. But it also made him look kind of silly, which was in a way the worst part, because it increased his self-consciousness. It's a pretty weird outfit all around, when you stop to think about it, like pajamas but with leprechaun pants and some very weird socks, and the fact that this particular one was soggy with sweat wasn't helping. Some guys, it is true, could look cool in a baseball uniform. But Mark Pang was not one of them. They'd had a hard time getting one that fit him; that was part of it.

That's why Raymond Powell, who played third base and who happened to be the coach's son, would sometimes call Mark Pang "Triple XL." That was a reference to the size of the jersey that had had to be special-ordered by McHenry's Sporting Goods from a place in Minneapolis. It looked a little different from everyone else's jersey, besides just being larger.

Raymond Powell had all sorts of mean nicknames for Mark Pang, like Lard-Ass, Ching-Chang, TOF, and POS. TOF stood for "tons of fun." POS stood for "piece of"— well, you know. Mark Pang couldn't bring himself to say it, even silently in his head. Raymond Powell was the meanest guy Mark Pang had ever run across in a lifetime of being hassled by mean guys. A lot of people liked him, though. Sometimes you'd even hear them say, when the subject of Raymond Powell came up, that he was a "nice guy." When you're good at baseball, you can get away with almost anything.

To hear Mark Pang's dad tell it, there weren't any guys like Raymond Powell around back when he was a kid playing baseball in the city. Baseball was everyone pulling together and loving the game and being enthusiastic when things went well and saying "We'll get 'em next year" when anyone screwed up. It sounded a lot more friendly, like an old movie or TV show, where everybody was always patting each other on the back and going, "Say, that'd be fine!" and "Hooray for baseball!" Either it really was like that back then, or his dad was lying. Or perhaps he had forgotten about the guys like Raymond Powell, just blocked them out of his mind. Mark Pang's dad seemed to have a blind spot about baseball. He had no concept of how difficult things could be for Mark Pang. After six innings of embarrassment and torture, Mark Pang's dad would say, "Fun game!" Or he would ask, "Hey, what are the guys doing after the game?" As though there was any chance that Raymond Powell and "the guys" would choose to hang around with Mark Pang when they weren't being forced to do so by the everybody-gets-to-play rules of the Lions League. Put it this way: Raymond Powell wasn't going to be patting Mark Pang on the back and saying "Hooray for baseball" any time soon.

But it was always a mistake to think about guys like Raymond Powell and your dad in these tense, impossible-square situations. It just made you more nervous, and that wasn't helping anybody.

Once Mark Pang had reached the impossible square and positioned himself as best he could, and provided he didn't trip over his cleats and tumble hilariously to the grass, there were three basic possibilities.

One: He could actually catch the ball, which would be amazing, just like in a movie. No one would be able to believe it. The odds were against him on that one, but stranger things had happened, though he couldn't actually think of one at the moment.

The second, far more likely possibility was that he would miscalculate the location of the impossible square, and end up standing in the wrong spot, holding his open mitt against the wrong patch of sky. The ball would fall harmlessly to the ground nearby, behind him or over to the side, and bounce (with any luck) to the zone of control of another player who would scoop it up and throw it to the second baseman. Everyone would laugh.

The third, most likely, and, it figured, worst possibility: He would catch the ball, but then drop it, or it would hit his mitt or some part of his body and bounce off. That was what everyone was expecting, and why half the spectators and everyone on the Green team began groaning in advance as soon as they saw the ball heading for center right. After that, Mark Pang would have to pick up the ball and throw it to the second baseman himself. Even if he managed to avoid freezing up and turning into a Mark Pang statue, there was still lots of room for tragedy. Mark Pang was a powerful but inaccurate thrower. Chances were he would overshoot second by a mile and the ball would wind up somewhere way over on the other side of the field. It was that special brand of Mark Pang magic. Zap! An easy out becomes a home run, before your very eyes. Boy, would the Green team and their nearest and dearest ever hate Mark Pang then. Raymond Powell would yell, "Pang, you piece of"—well, you know. Some of the dads would complain to the coach: Why do you put that kid out there? And Mark Pang's dad would be sitting in the stands, quietly disappointed and embarrassed even while trying to project a supportive attitude.

There was nothing in the world like Mark Pang's dad's face when he was experiencing baseball-related disappointment but trying to hide it by projecting a supportive attitude. It was really hard to take.

Once, talking to his mom, Mark Pang had floated the idea that it might work out better for all concerned if he tried some other activity next year for a change. Just to see what she would say. What she said was: "You can't quit baseball. It would kill your father—it's all he has to look forward to."

That seemed like an exaggeration, but maybe it wasn't much of one. Anyway, he sure didn't want that hanging over his head. Mark Pang's mom had added that his dad meant no harm, that he was doing the best he could, but that he just couldn't imagine an eleven-year-old boy not liking baseball. The phrase "not liking baseball" had no meaning to Mark Pang's dad. "Say that again," he would have had to say if anyone ever said "not liking baseball" to him. "I'm still not getting it."

But the thing was, liking baseball and being good at baseball weren't at all the same thing. In fact, Mark Pang liked baseball a lot. He loved going to ball games and watching them on TV. He liked talking about baseball. He liked hearing other people talk about baseball. Mark Pang was a huge Giants fan. He always wore his Giants cap, even though some kids would take advantage of that fact by drawing a parallel between the word *giant* and Mark Pang's size and weight. He even liked playing catch with his dad and going to the batting cages—he wasn't very good at either of those things, but it was okay and fun when the pressure was off and he didn't have to worry that he was going to ruin everybody's good time and get called names by Raymond Powell.

The way Mark Pang looked at it, there were almost three hundred million people in America, and maybe, say, one-third of them were baseball fans. Out of those hundred million people, there were quite a few who were good baseball players, certainly, but also a great many who were terrible, and possibly even some who were as bad as Mark Pang. One thing he knew: The vast majority of those hundred million people never spent *any* time actually playing baseball. They could walk around being baseball fans and no one would ever even know how bad they were at baseball. The subject never came up. Honestly, it seemed like a pretty good system, and he couldn't wait till the Green and the Dark Blue and Raymond Powell were far enough behind him that no one he met would be able to tell how unlikely it was that he would be able to field any balls that came his way.

Even Mark Pang's dad, who always walked around like he was Mr. Baseball or something, was never required by anyone to prove that he could actually play baseball. Of course, he had played a lot when he was a kid, and by all accounts he was pretty good. He was the first ever Chinese kid to make All City, back when he was in high school. But now all he did was watch television and eat sandwiches and say "At ease" and sit in a little cubicle working at a computer at work. He never had entire teams and their families and friends groaning and yelling at him in a public place. No one ever made him wear a hot, bulky, multi-layered, ill-fitting outfit featuring leprechaun pants and weird socks and a pajama-like jersey with "Pete's

Old-Fashion Italian Delicatessen" printed on it. People just took it as a given that he was good at baseball and everybody just got on with their lives.

But none of that was much help now. All in all, this had been just about the most stressful two and a half seconds of Mark Pang's life, and whether or not it would get even worse all depended on what happened next. Mark Pang stood in the impossible square with his mitt raised, the other hand behind it at the thumb part, squinting through the sweat that dripped steadily into his eyes, trying to tune out the screaming, focusing on the approaching ball, praying please God let me have this one.

"Sorry," he said, in advance. "Sorry, Dad."

M Sue Corbett **S**

POSITION: TEAM MOM | *ROOKIE YEAR: 2002

*BBI: 2

CAREER HIGHLIGHTS: Winner of the 2006 California Young Reader Medal for *12 Again*. (This is like being voted MVP of the junior high readers in California. At least, that's the way I look at it.)

FAVORITE TEAM: New York Mets

FAVORITE CURRENT PLAYER: Jose Reyes

FAVORITE PLAYER OF ALL TIME: Mookie Wilson

BEST GAME EVER: Game 6 of the 1986 World Series between the Mets and the Boston Red Sox.

*Stat key: BBI=Books Batted In (number of books published)
Rookie Year: first book published

FALL BALL
by Sue Corbett

1.

First practice for fall ball and I was late, screaming down the hill that led to Parkview, hoping not to hit a rock and be launched across my handlebars. I needed to talk to Carter, but by the time I threw my bike down behind the dugout, Coach Funda was already in the middle of one of his speeches.

"I can't carry this many guys on a fall team," he was saying as I slipped onto the bench. Did he look at me?

"This ain't T-ball anymore." He began to pace. When Funda starts wearing a path in the dirt, we're usually in for a lot of time on the pine. "If you're jes' here because your daddy thinks you're the next Chipper Jones, go on and break his fool heart now."

Then it hit me. What he was saying. "Wait a minute. You're not holding tryouts for *fall ball,* are you?"

"Thanks for making time in your busy schedule to join us, Kirby." He didn't answer the question.

"Is this a tryout?" I whispered to Gibson, next to me. Not that Gib had to worry. He could throw out runners from his knees and he could hit. Homers. The towering kind. He shrugged.

I quickly counted thirteen, fourteen other guys in the dugout, plus Jesse, our third baseman, leaning against the wall.

I glanced left down the bench. Next to Gib was Carter, our center fielder, whose mother had apparently been conspiring with mine to ruin our lives by signing us up for some cockamamie dance class. Trying to explain to her that there was a better chance of the Atlanta Braves putting me in their lineup than me going to Cotillion was why I was late in the first place.

The right side of our infield, Brendan and Brandon, were on Carter's left. Neither would be earning a Gold Glove during this lifetime, but they could slap the ball 'til it cried uncle. Brandon could also pitch. But most importantly, he could drool on command, dangling a string of saliva down past the letters on his uniform. Now, that is God-given talent. The fact that he's capitalized on this by, shall we say, leaving his mark on select pitches, only enhanced his chances of becoming a Parkview

Little League legend. His spot was totally secure.

At the far end of the bench sat another half-dozen kids I knew from playing with or against. And then there was Jesse, holding up the wall. Our best hitter. Also, a girl. The only girl in the whole league. There used to be another one, but she switched to softball in sixth grade.

This would be the four hundredth season in a row Jesse and I played together. We were best friends until third or fourth grade, when she locked hips with Kelly Carson and suddenly all they ever wanted to do was play teacher by making me do worksheets and giving me detention. Jesse's always been a better hitter than me, just like she's always been taller than me. But in the past year or two, she's pulled away in the hitting and the height departments.

Height is one of my shortcomings as an athlete, accent on *short*. Mom swears I'm gonna grow, but it seems like everybody has spurted but me.

"A great glove ain't enough at this level," Funda continued. The man could talk. "I'm looking for five-tool players."

"Screwdriver, hammer . . . ?" That was Brandon.

"Chainsaw!" Brendan added.

"Hitting for average, hitting for power, base-running . . ." Funda was ticking off tools on his fingers, but struggling with four and five. "Two more that have to do with fielding, which is a given. I'm looking for bats. Big bats. At this level, hitting beats pitching. Y'all know that. We need to get on base."

This time, he *definitely* looked at me, a black hole in the batting order. My average is hovering at about a buck-fifty. The Mendoza line would be an improvement.

"How many you gonna have on the team?" I asked.

"I got fourteen jerseys."

Sammy S. Sosa, he *was* gonna cut a couple of us. Me? Was he gonna cut *me*? This was fall ball! It was supposed to be a skill-building thing. No standings. No post-season. No pressure. I looked away as fast as I could and caught Jesse's eye. She mouthed, *"Don't worry."* Easy for her to say.

"You and you and you," Funda said, gesturing with his finger. "Get bats and helmets. Eveybody else, find a spot in the field."

He did not point at me.

2.

I trudged out to short. Fall has always been my favorite time to play baseball. People who are not baseball people think Little League begins in raw spring and ends in August, but that's the regular season. Fall ball is for gamers. The springtime posers have gone off to play soccer, an alleged sport in which you can't use your hands and people deliberately get hit in the head. We use our hands, and if the ball hits us, we get a base, not a concussion.

It's just the real baseball players here come September.

I sized up Davis Hollander as he trotted out to right. No taller than me, maybe even shorter. I had a cheery thought: Maybe he can't hit either! Then I'd just need one other person to demonstrate a tremendously bad attitude, or reveal symptoms of a chronic disease— tuberculosis? leprosy?—during tryouts. That wasn't asking too much, was it? I toed the dirt with my cleat to smooth my spot.

It wasn't always like this. I used to be on base constantly. When you're learning to pitch, the strike zone is tougher to find than the Bermuda Triangle. I had patience, and I was rewarded with walk after walk after walk.

Also, I can bunt, and I will. One strike and I drop the bat and place it. I'm not the fastest sneaker in the shoe store, but you don't need Jose Reyes's speed in the early years of Little League, because fielding is still only a concept. Even if the ball is picked cleanly, nine of ten throws go into the outfield. I've stretched bunts into inside-the-park home runs.

But a year ago, I saw my first curveball. Well, *saw* is not the right word. I didn't see it at all. A ball came out of Jackson Marbury's throwing hand but by the time it crossed the plate, it had vanished from the spot where it was supposed to be.

Swoosh.

Swoosh.

Swoosh.

Sit down.

It wasn't only me that day. Jackson struck out eleven. But eventually Jesse and Carter and the others figured it out.

I haven't. And I'm worried I never will. Last month, the score was tied in the final inning of a playoff game at Hampton. Jesse was on first, Brendan at the plate. I was in the on-deck circle when Funda motioned me back to the dugout.

"Have a seat, little man. I gotta give K.J. a turn."

Keenan Jacob Myers is our fourth outfielder. He can't tell a cutoff man from Mr. Potato Head, but he goes up there hacking like swings are on sale and the store is on fire.

"But, Funda, who's gonna play short in the bottom of the inning?"

"I'm not gonna worry about that if we score a bunch of runs right now, Kirb."

I slumped onto the bench. Can you imagine? Being pulled in the late innings of a playoff game?

Brendan drew a walk. K.J. blooped a Texas Leaguer into shallow right. Jesse scored from second without a throw.

I'm pretty sure K.J. hit a curveball.

3.

"What's with you?" Jesse asked as we jogged off the field for our turn at the plate.

"Think I'll get cut?"

She sighed. "You know what your problem is?" She took off her cap, tightened her ponytail, and then threaded it through the hole in the back again.

"I think too much?"

"Exactly."

"You've mentioned that before."

"You wanna use my bat?" She was pulling on her gloves while I tried to find a helmet that didn't look like a family of lice had made a home for themselves inside it.

"Does it have any hits in it for me?"

"Kirby, look around. You see another shortstop here?"

"You. You could probably play short."

"Kirby, that is *your* dirt."

"Until a shortstop who can hit shows up. Then, poof. Instant eviction. 'Mr. O'Leary, have your stuff at the curb by sundown.'"

"O'Leary! Stop flirting and get in the box." Funda calling. I squashed the helmet down over my ears and hoped for the best.

"You been working in the cage, like I told you?" He reached into a five-gallon pail of baseballs he had beside him on the mound.

"Yessir." This wasn't technically true, but I had been

doing push-ups. A hundred a day. My biceps now had a firm marble-sized knot, as opposed to the previous pea-sized knot.

I stood in and he lobbed a few easy tosses down the middle of the plate. I actually made contact with one, which dribbled almost to his feet before he gloved it. "Kirby, you're doing it again. I don't wanna see your head come up until that ball is skipping into the outfield, got it?"

I nodded and licked my lips. Head down.

"And you're still stepping toward third. Step toward me. *Into* the ball, not *away* from the ball."

"Got it." Head down. In, not away. Keep your eye on it. Extend your arms. Shift your weight. Drive it through your hands. Got it. Got it. Got it. I felt a headache coming on. Maybe the helmet was too small. My brain felt squeezed.

The next pitch was a curve. I kept my head down with my eye on it until I could extend my arms and drive it through my hands. I know I did because I had a perfectly clear view of it as the ball whooshed directly under my bat and thudded into Gib's glove. Funda threw me six more with consistent results.

"Cripes, Kirby. What am I going to do with you? Jesse, c'mon. Show him how it's done. Kirby, I want you to watch exactly what she does and then go home and practice it in the mirror until you can do it in your sleep. You got that?"

I nodded and handed Jesse her bat as we crossed paths. "You'll get 'em next time, Kirb."

I grunted. Was this it? Was my baseball career gonna end at age twelve?

Carter patted me on the head when I sat down next to him in the dugout. "Could be worse," he said. "He could've told you to memorize Gib's swing."

"What's wrong with that?"

"I'd rather look at Jesse."

"Why?"

"Whaddya mean, why? Is there something you want to share with your best friend, Kirb? *Would* you rather look at Gib?"

Just then I remembered I needed to talk to him. "Carter, tell me it's not true that you signed up for this 'Cotillion' thing."

"The dancing lessons?"

"My mother said I had to do it because you were doing it."

"Well, my mother said *you* signed up and didn't want to go by yourself."

Precisely what I thought. Collusion.

4.

I planned to tell my mother I was on to her the moment I got home. She was waiting for me, smiling like she'd just been named Peanut Festival Queen, holding something on a hanger covered with a plastic bag.

"Got you a present, Kirby," she said, all cheerful-like.

"What is it, dry cleaning? You got me dry cleaning? Aw, Mom, you shouldn't have."

She arched an eyebrow, which is her way of calling me a wise guy. My mother can say more with an eyebrow than most people can with an entire language at their disposal. "A new suit. Your *first* suit."

"Oh, joy. What's that in the pocket? A gift certificate for a root canal?"

"Put it on, you rascal. The pants need hemming."

She was right about that. The fabric crumpled in folds around my feet. The jacket fit, since I have my father's gorilla arms. My knuckles practically scrape the sidewalk, giving me the coveted Freak of Nature look so many desire but cannot hope to attain—spaghetti arms with leg stubs.

My mother came in as I was admiring myself. She put the little bench my sister uses to reach the sink down in front of the mirror. "Step up, Mr. O'Leary."

"Do I really have to wear this monkey suit?"

"Wucky you're not a girl," she said, tacking up a hem with straight pins she had wedged between her lips. "They haff to wear white gluffs."

I toppled off the bench, tripping on the pants and impaling myself on a pin. "Ouch! Mom!" I hopped on my good leg while I pulled the pin out of my flesh. "You didn't say there'd be girls at this thing!"

My mother laughed, which was not only insensitive but dangerous when you have pins in your mouth. "Du are poffibwee da densest stwaight-A student on the pwanet, Kirby." She took the pins out. "Were you planning to tango with Carter?"

Oh, man. Girls. "What kind of dancing is this? I mean, are we going to have to, y'know . . . touch?"

"Don't worry. They'll be wearing gloves."

That was twice in one day somebody told me not to worry.

It wasn't working.

5.

"See? You're starting at short." Jesse jabbed a finger on the clipboard hanging in the dugout. "As usual."

I was retying my cleats before our first game. "Only because Davis Hollander decided he'd rather get hit in the head." He'd signed up for soccer. A warm breeze blew through the dugout, ruffling Funda's lineup.

"Can't you just be happy?"

"I am happy." I forced a grin. "It's just . . ." Out on the field, Gibson was warming up Brandon. Carter and Nick Dressler were in short center, throwing a ball in a high arc between them. It was a perfect day. The sun was out but not punishing like it is in July and August, when sometimes you have to choose between losing sight of a pop-up or scorching the top layer of your corneas.

"Just what?"

"It's just that the end is near, Jess. It's coming. And I always thought I was going to be a baseball player. I mean, my whole life, that's what I was planning for."

"Not true, Kirb. Remember Career Day at Peas and Carrots Preschool?"

"You obviously do."

"You said you were going to be a helicopter when you grew up."

"Turns out that's more realistic." I swatted her with my glove to get her to follow me to the infield. I didn't want to think about the end of my baseball career anymore. About how I only made Funda's team because one kid withdrew his name and another wet his pants every time the pitch was high and inside. I just wanted to play.

In the third inning, I even got on base, leaning in on a pitch that kept sinking and turning in on itself until—bingo!—it plunked me on the toe. Take your base, batter. A walk and an infield single to load the bases, and then, boom, Jesse went yard, clearing every duck from the pond.

As days go, it missed achieving perfection only because that night I had to go to Cotillion, a.k.a, Modern Torture for Southern Boys.

There were other guys from school there. Some girls too, but it took a while to figure that out because they were barely recognizable. Their hair was all glossy and curled, and they were wearing high heels, making me shorter than ever.

The lady in charge, Mrs. Dinwiddie, wore a sequined gown and carried a cordless mike. A disco ball rotated, throwing little checkerboard squares of light around the room. Along one wall, a table held a punch bowl and cups. I got thirsty the moment I saw it.

"Ladies and gentlemen," Mrs. Dinwiddie began. She had that sugary voice teachers use to tell you there's a term paper due the first day back from Christmas vacation. "Please form two lines and we shall begin."

"Showtime," Carter said. He had a new suit too, and I think he was wearing cologne! What is *happening* to him?

There was about six feet of space between our line and the girls', but I avoided eye contact by studying first my shoes, then Mrs. Dinwiddie. She had really tall hair. It was more like architecture than hair. She had white gloves too, only hers went all the way past her elbows. Weird.

"Cotillion is more than dancing," she chirped. "It is etiquette education. Having good manners is a necessity in today's society. So we will begin tonight by introducing ourselves to the lady or gentleman across the aisle."

Carter strode right over to Mary Kay Childress, the girl across from him. The girl across from me was a stranger. I gave her a parade wave. Then I looked at my shoes. My mother must have polished them. They were as shiny as the girls' hair.

"Very good," Mrs. Dinwiddie said, *finally,* getting people to wrap up their introductions. What could they possibly be saying to each other? "Now we will begin with the quadrille."

"What century have we been transported to?" I asked Carter.

"Check it out," he said, nodding toward the far end of the girls' line.

"Holy crap." Swearing is probably not proper etiquette but it just came out. The person Carter was pointing out was . . . Jesse.

"Jesse is *hot,*" he said.

"Jesse is not hot, you idiot. She's our third baseman."

"Too bad baseball's not a contact sport, huh, Kirb?"

I was actually relieved when the music started, because I was sure my face had turned a shade of red most often seen at a fruit stand. I swiveled my head for another look as I attempted to box step with my partner. Jesse was wearing a blue dress with straps so thin they would snap in two if she went horizontal to make a diving stop deep in the hole. That thought made my face go red again. And she was wearing dangly earrings! Was this was one of the seven signs of the apocalypse?

At Cotillion, you switch dancing partners more

often than the Tampa Bay Devil Rays change pitchers, so before long the girl facing me was Jesse. For the first time ever, I wasn't sure what to say to her.

"Nice homer today."

"Way to take one for the team, Kirb. Catching it on your toe like that? What's your on-base percentage now?"

I used to be able to tell everyone what their OBP was, immediately after their at-bat. I could do the calculations in my head. At one point in those kid-pitch years, I had a staggering .475 OBP. By way of comparison, let me just say that Andruw Jones's OBP the year he should've won the MVP was .452. "I stopped keeping track of that when it sunk into double digits."

"Sorry. Shouldn't have brought it up."

The music started. Mrs. Dimwitted was fox-trotting. I was shuffling. The fox-trot was a relief, because it didn't involve much hand-to-body contact. The fabric of Jesse's dress looked slippery. I might accidentally touch something important. I was sweating profusely. In fact, my body seemed to be working to make me suffer on as many levels as possible, because suddenly I got an intense craving to eat.

"I know this sounds strange, but do you smell jelly donuts?" I asked.

"It's my perfume. I mean, I borrowed it from my mom."

"Your mom wears Jelly Donut perfume?"

"It's vanilla oil. But I know what you mean. When she wears it I always think I smell sugar cookies."

Yum. It smelled delicious. I stepped closer before stopping myself from doing what I was about to do. I WAS ABOUT TO SNIFF JESSE BRYANT!

GET ME OUTTA HERE!

6.

Cotillion had affected Carter deeply. He started calling Funda "sir," and the rest of us by our last names, as in, "After you, Mr. O'Leary," which he said to me as we lined up for BP before Saturday's game.

"Put a sock in it, if you please," I told him.

"You two gonna bat or just keep jabbering?" Jesse had sidled up behind us.

Carter stepped out of the on-deck circle. "Ladies first."

Jesse looked at me for an explanation and—apparently, this is a special girl talent—arched her eyebrow the same way my mother does.

I shrugged. "He thinks they're giving out grades in etiquette education."

BP didn't do me any good. On the field, I was the lead man on three—count 'em—three double plays, but all Funda will remember is that I struck out twice.

"You can't get a hit with that bat sound asleep on your shoulder, Kirby."

I didn't respond.

"Can you meet me halfway and at least take a swing?"

"The pitch was outside!" A little. Maybe. I put my bat in the rack with more force than necessary. "If Major League Baseball can have a designated hitter, why can't we have a designated fielder?" I asked, loudly, before planting my seat on the bench. Gibson scooted away from me, as if weak hitting might be contagious. "Wouldn't that LEVEL THE PLAYING FIELD?"

"Is this gonna be a speech?" Brendan asked.

I looked at him to respond but saw Brandon first. He was drooling.

"Oh, forget it." He was trying to cheer me up but it wasn't gonna work.

Then I had to go to Cotillion. Again.

7.

Mrs. Dumbwaiter was wearing a fringed vest and cowboy boots.

"Did I miss a memo?" I asked Carter. "I thought the steer wrestling was next weekend."

"Tonight we have a real treat—a Western theme!" she sang into her mike. "Let's start with an all-time favorite—'The Cotton-Eyed Joe.'"

"Yeehaw," I said, to no one. Carter had already linked arms with Mary Kay.

All that swinging your partner parches the throat,

so, first chance I got, I headed to the punch bowl and ladled out some mystery liquid, careful to scoop around the floating orange slices.

"Good game today, Kirb."

I knew it was Jesse without turning around. I smelled jelly donuts.

"Good game for you." She'd gone two for three with two RBIs.

"Hey, we won."

"Not because of me."

She took a long sip. "You're scared up there, Kirby. The pitcher smells it."

"Can I borrow your vanilla oil? Maybe instead of fear he'd smell jelly donuts and once we get him thinking about food, he'll accidentally lob me a meatball."

She arched an eyebrow. "Have you thought about meditation?"

"Aren't you the one who keeps telling me to stop thinking?"

"Baseball is supposed to be fun, Kirb."

I nearly spit out my punch, an etiquette violation that probably carries the death penalty. "FUN? It's not FUN, Jesse. It's my life. I can't imagine not playing baseball."

She snorted. "Lucky you're not a girl, then."

"What do white gloves have to do with this?"

"Kirby, are all braniacs as dumb as you? I mean, think about it. Are there any girls on the high school team? Have you checked the Braves' roster recently? Guys, Kirby, all guys."

"You can play softball."

"I don't want to play softball."

"It's not like they're forcing you to play soccer."

"You're as bad as my parents." She refilled her cup. "What if somebody told you, for no reason you had any control over, you couldn't play, even if you darn well *could* play. Better than a lot of boys."

I sipped my punch, thinking. "That would suck. I mean, maybe someday I will finally grow, but I guess there's no hope you'll grow out of being a girl."

"No. No hope at all." She swigged the rest of her punch, then nodded toward the dance floor. "You want to dosey-do?"

"Sure." It was the least I could do.

8.

Later that week, I was in science lab when it struck me. Jesse and I had biology problems. My body was betraying me, stalling on the growth spurt thing, but there was a slim chance I could hang on long enough for my body to catch up with my brain's plans for it. Jesse's problem was unconquerable.

Why was she still playing?

Because she loved it. You could see it in her batting stance. Her intensity. Her singular focus on clobbering the ball. The way she ran the bases like her hair was on fire. I had been thinking about what Carter said, about Jesse being hot. But the prettiest thing about Jesse was the way she played the game. Easy. Cool. Confident.

No wonder she was still playing. Nobody would give up something they loved like that without a fight.

Saturday, my mother was outside raking leaves in the backyard when I went to get my bike. "You coming to the game?" I asked.

She leaned on her rake. "I thought I made you nervous."

"Turns out, *I* make me nervous."

She pulled another strand into her big pile. "Kirby, maybe you should have quit before it stopped being fun."

Fun? Is that all people think baseball is? "I can't bring myself to quit now."

She came over and gave me an arm-around-the-shoulder hug, which we had negotiated as the only permissible public display of affection. "I'll be over as soon as I finish this. Wanna jump in the pile?"

My first reaction was to scoff, but then I remembered Jesse and I used to love hurtling ourselves into a mountain of dead leaves.

"Nah, but thanks," I said. "Maybe later."

9.

At the game, I made an excellent, if I do say so myself, grab with my meat hand in the third, saving two runs from scoring. The impact almost broke two fingers, but it was worth it.

My first turn at bat came in the bottom of the inning. Frickin' Jackson Marbury had set us down in order so far, but we had a rally building with nobody out, one on, and a three-and-oh count to Nick. I was on deck when Jesse motioned me back to the dugout.

"Put out your wrist," she ordered.

"Why?"

"Just do it. Quick." Before I could object, she grabbed my arm and spritzed me. The air filled with the scent of jelly donuts.

"Are you trying to get me killed?!"

"Shhh! Steer clear of Brandon. This is sure to start him drooling."

Nick walked and I was up.

"Okay, let's put the ball in play, Kirb," Funda called.

A nauseatingly familiar sense of dread settled over me as I walked to the plate. I was beginning to see my baseball future clearly, and the picture showed me sitting in the stands. Out of baseball at thirteen. Watching the Braves on TV, pretending the high school didn't have a team, even when they were winning and Carter's and Gibson's pictures were in the newspaper.

The first pitch was, you guessed it, Uncle Charlie. It

was heading directly into my kitchen when the bottom dropped out of it.

"Keep yer eye on it, Kirby!" Funda.

The wind swept some dirt from the backstop toward the mound. Over the outfield fence, the last of this year's leaves rained on cars in the parking lot. I took a deep breath and reminded myself that Jackson Marbury was flunking algebra and I could bust quadratic equations in my sleep. I ground my heel into the dirt and gave him my death stare.

Then, I swear, I saw him sniff the air. A look of confusion crossed his face. He shook his head and set. I nearly cracked up and I had to stop myself from looking into the dugout to see if Jesse noticed it too.

Jesse. Would she be pretending the high school team didn't exist too? Would they make an exception for her? Would she finally cave and play softball?

Funda gave me the signs from third. "Level swing, Kirb, level swing." He clapped his hands.

I waggled my bat, waiting.

Jesse would find a way to play. And if she could, with her insurmountable biological problem, couldn't I too? Okay, maybe I wasn't going to be a major leaguer, but our high school team isn't even that good! Were the years I spent shagging flies and fielding choppers wasted? Didn't hard work count for anything anymore? Didn't dreams?

The ball came hurtling at me but I saw the seams

twisting. I swung my gorilla arms with pendulum force just as the ball was about to swoon below my waist.

It skipped into the grass in deep left center. I was pulling into second before the outfielder got it out of his glove.

I wanted to jump up and down. I wanted to scream, "See?! I can do it!" Instead, I pretended I had done this before. I might never do it again, but at the moment, that didn't matter.

I looked into the dugout for Jesse. She gave me a smile as wide as the bill on her cap. Carter was right. Jesse was hot. My knee buckled, probably, y'know, from running so fast to second. But then a thought hit me like a line drive in the gullet: Girls were another kind of curveball. I started to worry about that until I remembered what Jesse was always telling me: Don't think. Just react. So I smiled back and then, I can still hardly believe I did this, but . . . I winked at her.

And that girl winked right back at me.

POSITION: RIGHT FIELD | *ROOKIE YEAR: 2005

*BBI: Just one so far. *Defining Dulcie* (Dial 2006). But I'm aiming for the fences!

ROOKIE YEAR: My first visit to the big leagues happened in 2005 with a short story in the collection *Every Man for Himself* (Dial 2005).

CAREER HIGHLIGHTS: February 15, 2006: first fan letter for *Defining Dulcie*! As far as ball games, I did once save the day by catching a high fly at the fence in the final inning of a just-for-fun softball league without dropping (or choking on) a two-stick cherry Popsicle.

FAVORITE TEAM: Oakland A's

FAVORITE PLAYER: It's a close tie between Jimmy Morris (as played by Dennis Quaid in *The Rookie*) and Crash Davis (as played by Kevin Costner in *Bull Durham*).

BEST GAME EVER: In my son's first Little League game ever, he stepped up to the plate and smacked a line drive over the head of the opposing pitcher and second baseman. As he sprinted around the bases for a stand-up triple, I jumped up and down with so much enthusiasm that I knocked a nearby dad off the edge of the grandstand. It wasn't so far a fall that the guy got hurt, but it was a little too far for me to jump down and help him up. Plus I didn't want to miss the end of the play. I don't remember who won the game.

GREAT MOMENTS IN BASEBALL

by Paul Acampora

When my mother and I step through the gate at Harvey DeCamillo Memorial Baseball Field, my brother Jeffrey is already on the mound. He's pitching for Dubois Plumbing. This afternoon, Jeffrey is leading the Plumbers against Little League powerhouse Sal's Grinders. Jeffrey swivels his head to check a runner on first. That's when he sees me.

He stops. He smiles. He waves.

I roll my eyes. *"Play the game,"* I mouth at him.

He grins and turns back to the plate.

"Jennifer," Mom calls to me from the bottom of the bleachers, "let's go to the top."

"Fine," I say.

Summer has nearly rolled into fall, so the air has

a bit of cool in it. The place smells like hot dogs and spilled Cokes and dry grass. I turn and follow Mom up the bleachers near the first-base line. The wooden benches creak and moan beneath my mother's pink dollar-store flip-flops. I don't need to look around to see that she is the largest human in the park. Jeffrey and I estimate that our mother's feet carry about a thousand pounds each.

"Come on, Jeffrey!" Mom manages to yell after she catches her breath at the top of the stands. "Dig in that toe. Crack that whip!"

Despite her satin Boston Red Sox jacket, a few good lines, and the just-right way she's learned to pull a ponytail through the back of her cap, Mom knows more about pitching a fit than hitting a cutoff man. That doesn't stop her from providing a running commentary on the game. "Will you look at your brother," Mom says to me. "He stares at his feet like he's got some great big arsenal to choose from. All he's got is a fastball and half a curve."

"Mmmm," I say. I want to give Jeffrey and the Plumbers the benefit of the doubt. But honestly, I think the best thing Dubois Plumbing has going for them this season is their name. *Dooo-bwah.* I just love saying it. "Go Dubois! Dooobwah! Doobwah-Doobwah-Dooobwah!"

Mom shoots me a disgusted look. The umpire behind the plate calls, "Ball two." The Dubois catcher tosses the ball back to Jeffrey, and Mom yells, "You're blind!" I don't know if she's talking to the umpire, the catcher, or me.

Down on the mound, Jeffrey brings the ball behind his back. His fingers fumble around the seams, and he's flexing his wrist like he's going to turn a doorknob, not throw a pitch. My brother's got our father's dark hair and his tall lanky build. Every once in a while Jeffrey actually looks like a baseball player, but of course, looks can be deceiving.

"He's going to try that wishball," I say.

"The slider?" asks Mom.

"He wishes."

I used to be a pretty good Little League pitcher. Dad gave me my first pitching lesson when I was nine. I was all gawky legs and long arms. My hair, the same stringy blond as Mom's, kept flying out of my cap and covering up my face. I've cut it short since then. And I'm too old for Little League now. But if you saw me on the mound today, you could tell right away that I still know what I'm doing. I've got a textbook delivery—good launch position, great rotation, and solid footwork. I've got a snap on the end of my release that can make your ears ring. I work out with Jeffrey in the backyard almost every day. I've got to do it because our dad died almost three years ago, when I was twelve and Jeffrey was eight. That's when Mom decided to declare herself queen of baseball.

"Jennifer," Jeffrey said to me back then. "Nothing against Mom, but I'd rather play alone than practice with her. She gets all crazy."

"I'll play with you," I promised. Baseball is not the sort of thing you can do alone. If you do, it's a sad, pointless, hollow sort of game.

"Ball three!" calls the ump.

"Damn," says Mom.

Dad would be so proud just to see Jeffrey in uniform. I mean, it's not like my brother is wearing Yankee pinstripes or something, but the monkey wrench on the Dubois Plumbing cap is a nice touch.

Tock!

A Grinder boy gets a big piece of Jeffrey's half a curve. The baseball leaps into the air. It sails over the second baseman. It's still rising when it clears the outfield. We all hear it *thud* into the parking lot gravel. "Wow," says somebody in the stands.

"Damn," Mom says again.

"Baseball has everything," Dad used to tell us. "Grace, speed, patience, drama. It's the perfect game." To hear him talk, you'd think Jesus and his mother were upstairs stitching covers on new balls. Thankfully, the drama of the current inning ends quickly when Sal's next batter fouls Jeffrey's first pitch into the Dubois Plumbing catcher's mitt.

"You're out!" yells the ump.

"Thank God," says Mom.

Jeffrey smiles like he made that happen on purpose. He waves at us as he jogs toward the dugout.

"You want a hot dog?" Mom asks me.

"Why don't you just ask me if I want a cigar? They have about the same nutritional value."

"You want a cigar?" she asks.

"Just a Diet Coke, please."

"Diet Coke?" says Mom. "Why don't you just get a big cup full of kerosene? They have about the same nutritional value."

I hate it when she's right. "Never mind," I say. "I'll get it."

My mother and I didn't get along all that well even before Dad died. I don't know why I've always felt the need to cross her. It's usually not worth it, and sometimes it can be sort of scary. I step down the bleachers toward the snack stand, and I think back to when I was in the fourth grade at St. Joseph Elementary School. I stuffed a spitball into a milk straw and launched it at the crucifix above the blackboard. This wasn't like a big religious statement on my part or anything. It's just that the cross made a great target. So Jesus hung there all afternoon with a spitball on his belly button. The next day our teacher, Sister Agnes, discovered what had happened. And who was responsible. She marched me to the front of the room and pointed to Christ's navel. "THIS. IS. TERRIBLE," she declared. "Terrible! So bad that last night . . . last night, God caused a plane to crash in the Andes."

The class gasped.

"Boys and girls," Sister continued, "twenty-four people died in that crash." She turned to me. "I hope you have learned your lesson."

"Yes, Sister," I said. And all of a sudden, my throat felt like I'd swallowed gasoline. I mean, what if God actually makes world management decisions based on the stuff we do? That afternoon, I cried the entire bus ride home. "I'm a murderer. I'm a murderer. I'm a murderer." Mom met me at the bus stop, and I rushed into her arms wailing, "I'm a murderer!"

"What the hell?" she said.

I explained what I had done, and she tossed me into the backseat of our brown Plymouth Duster. Sister Agnes was still in the classroom when Mom dragged me back through the door. "Sister Agnes," said Mom, "Jennifer explained to me that she caused an airliner to crash."

"Mrs. Baxter," Sister Agnes began.

Mom held up her hand. I recognized the gesture as the international sign for *Shut up or I'm going to smack you.* Sister Agnes must have recognized it too because she stopped talking. "Sister," Mom continued. "You are going to tell my child that she is not a murderer, and then you are going to apologize."

Sister Agnes hesitated.

Mom stepped forward so that her face nearly brushed

the nun's habit. "Say you're sorry," Mom said, "or the sky will rain airplanes tonight."

Sister Agnes apologized. I finished fourth grade at the public school.

When I get back to the stands, Mom is yelling at the pitcher for Sal's Grinders. "You stink! Slo-Pitch was last night! My daughter throws better than you!"

"That's really nice, Mom." Of course that last part is true.

Mom ignores me. Jeffrey's standing at the plate with a too-big bat in his hand. He's looking at a full count, and Sal's pitcher delivers a fat fastball right down the middle.

"Strike!" yells the umpire. Jeffrey goes down looking.

"Dammit!" hollers Mom. "Dammit! That was not a strike! Dammit!" She stomps her feet and screams, "You suck, ref! You suck!"

"That was a strike, Mom." I don't bother adding that there are no refs in baseball.

"You could work with him a little more," she snaps.

"I do work with him," I say. "On his pitching. Not his hitting." I never was much of a hitter.

"Why don't you teach him your changeup?" Mom asks irritably.

"It's not mine. Dad showed it to me."

I see a flash of red cross my mother's face. I don't know if it's anger or surprise or what. I know that she hasn't forgiven our father for wrapping his car around a tree, and I think she hates it when I remind her that Jeffrey and I were not hatched from eggs. That there actually used to be somebody we called Dad.

Jeffrey peeks out of the dugout and gives us yet another wave. Except for his complete lack of athletic ability, he's so much like our father it's crazy. He's funny and easygoing and just happy to be alive.

"Are you nervous?" I asked Jeffrey earlier when he was getting ready for the game.

"What is there to be nervous about? We're the worst team in the league. We haven't beat anybody all year." He laughed. "We're probably not going to."

"Don't you want to win?"

"Sure." He pulled an old box of baseball cards from beneath his bed. "But I think we'd have to call this a no-pressure situation."

I thought of something Dad used to say: If you fall out of an airplane without a parachute, go ahead and enjoy the view.

Jeffrey found a card in his collection. "Ever hear about Silvio Garcia?" he asked. He didn't wait for me to answer. "He was almost the first black player in the majors."

"You have a card for the almost-first black player in the majors?"

He shook his head and showed me the baseball card. "This is Branch Rickey."

I gave my brother a blank look.

"In 1945, the Brooklyn Dodgers decided that they were going to bring a black player into the majors. They heard of this guy, Silvio Garcia. He was an all-star shortstop in Cuba, and let me tell you, Jen. Those guys can really play."

"Wasn't Jackie Robinson the first black player in the majors?"

"That came later. But first . . . " Jeffrey waved the baseball card in my face. "Branch Rickey, president of the Dodgers, flew down to Havana to meet Silvio Garcia. Branch Rickey asked Silvio, 'What would you do if a white American slapped your face?'"

"What did Señor Garcia say?" I asked.

"He said, 'I kill him.'"

"Silvio Garcia." I said it again slowly. "Sillllvio Garrrrcia . . . I like him. Did he every play in the big leagues?"

Jeffrey shook his head. "I don't think he really wanted to."

"Why not?"

"Maybe that's not why he played the game, Jen. Maybe he just played for . . . " Jeffrey hesitated.

"For what?"

"You know," my brother said. Then he repeated something Dad used to tell us. "Baseball is a game of great moments. Maybe Silvio Garcia just played for the great moments."

All of a sudden I felt all choked up with missing my father. And I loved my little brother so much I didn't know what to do with it all. "Oh," is all I could say.

"Of course, telling Branch Rickey where to get off must have been a pretty great moment."

"Yeah." I took a big breath. "How about giving me a real great moment?"

"Silvio Garcia was real."

"You know what I mean."

Jeffrey hopped to his feet. My brother may not have a changeup or a slider or much of a curve, but he does have an encyclopedia of baseball stories in his head. He writes them down on index cards, including details of the plays plus the word-for-word announcers' calls of what, in Jeffrey's opinion, are the greatest moments in baseball.

"Game one of the 1988 World Series. Kirk Gibson hobbles up to the plate."

"Not that one," I said. "And don't give me the ground ball to Billy Buckner either." Dad was a lifelong Red Sox fan. On the off chance that he looks in on us now and then from the afterlife, I didn't want to make him relive the most painful Red Sox moment of all time.

Jeffrey thought for a second. "Okay," he said. "October third, 1951. The Polo Grounds. New York Giants versus Brooklyn Dodgers. Bottom of the ninth in game three of a three-game playoff." He started to get into it. "Bobby Thomson's at the plate for the Giants. Runners on second and third. Giants are down four to two. Brooklyn's Ralph Branca's on the mound." Jeffrey put on his best announcer voice. "Hartung down the line at third, not taking any chances. Lockman without too big of a lead at second—but he'll be running like the wind if Thomson hits one. Branca throws . . . There's a long drive. It's going to be . . . I BELIEVE . . . THE GIANTS WIN THE PENNANT! THE GIANTS WIN THE PENNANT! THE GIANTS WIN THE PENNANT! THE GIANTS WIN THE PENNANT! And they're going CRAZY! THEY'RE GOING CRAZY! OH HO!" Now my brother and I were jumping up and down like maniacs. THE GIANTS WIN THE PENNANT! THE GIANTS WIN THE PENNANT!

"Hey!" Mom yelled from downstairs. "Knock it off!"

Jeffrey and I stopped and looked at each other. We still had big, dumb pumpkin grins on our faces. "Wow," I said. "That was great."

"Yeah." Jeffrey laughed. He slipped the baseball cards back under his bed.

"You ever notice," I said, "that sometimes baseball's greatest moments are a pitcher's worst nightmare?"

"Nope." Jeffrey gathered up his cap and pitcher's glove. "I never did."

I wonder if Jeffrey's thinking about the nightmare scenario right now. On the Harvey DeCamillo mound, he's in the last inning and somehow, Dubois Plumbing is holding on to a six to four lead. At the same time, Sal's boys are trying to rally. They have runners on first and third, but there's two outs. Jeffrey is trying to stare down Scotty Hardek, Sal's best player and the league's top hitter.

"Walk him," Mom yells. "Get the next guy, Jeffrey. Walk him!"

I look at Mom. I look at Jeffrey. I know Mom is right, but I can't help myself. I scream, "Strike him out, Jeffrey! Mow that kid down!"

Mom turns to me. "What are you talking about? That's nonsense."

"Big KO!" I yell to my brother. "You can do it!"

Jeffrey glances my way. He gives me a silly grin.

"This is a baseball game!" Mom hollers. "There are right choices and wrong choices. Pitching to that guy is the wrong choice."

"Doo-bwah!" I cheer. "Doobwah! Doobwah! Doobwah!"

Jeffrey glances toward the dugout. I see the bored Plumbers coach shrug and then give my brother the thumbs-up. Pitch away!

"Oh, come on," Mom says. "He's going to get pounded!"

"Get him, little bro!"

Jeffrey goes into his windup and tries the slider again. This time, it actually works!

"Strike!" shouts the umpire.

Mom stands. "I can't watch this," she says. "I'm walking home without you."

"Will you please cheer or shut up," I say before I can stop my mouth.

"Strike two!" yells the umpire.

"All right!" Mom and I yell together. Now we're jumping up and down on the rickety bleachers. Mom has those wooden stands bouncing and rocking like an Olympic diving board. People around us are actually changing seats. "Come on, Jeffrey!" we yell. "One more!"

I look at the kid at the plate, and I just know he's waiting for a fastball. "Curve, curve, curve," I chant under my breath, but the minute Jeffrey goes into his windup, I see the fastball coming. "No," I shout. But it's too late.

TOCK!

A few moments later . . . *THUD*. The ball lands on a bright red minivan parked near the Tiny Tots playground all the way across the street. I've never seen anybody smack a ball that far out of Harvey DeCamillo. "Whoa," I say. And it's game over. Grinders win 7–6.

Mom sinks down on the bench and glares at me. "I hope you're happy."

I take a big breath before I get possessed by the spirit of Silvio Garcia and say something reckless. "I'm happy enough," I tell her.

We work our way down the bleachers toward the

field. Jeffrey's shaking hands with everybody, Plumbers and Grinders alike. When he sees Mom and me, he tucks his glove under his arm and jogs our way "You were awesome," I say. "That was the best batter in the league. You had him down oh and two."

Jeffrey grins. "Thanks."

"I'm going to teach you that changeup this week," I tell him. "You had that Grinder kid almost the whole way. Right, Mom?"

Our mother just shakes her head. I can tell she's angry. "Jeffrey," she finally says. "You could have won that game."

"It's all right," my brother says.

"Here," says Mom. She shoves a couple bills into Jeffrey's hand. "Take your know-it-all sister out for an ice cream. I'm going home."

"Don't you want to come?" Jeffrey asks.

Mom raises her hand and waves at us as she walks away. "You two deserve each other."

Jeffrey and I stand on the little stone bridge that runs between the gravel parking lot and the baseball field. We watch our mother march away, her head down, her flip-flops kicking up little clouds of dust. I turn and look over the side of the bridge.

"Don't worry about her," Jeffrey says to me.

I keep staring off the bridge. I am so angry at our mother that I want to vomit, and I miss Dad so much that tears burn down my face. To see me concentrate on the trickle of water limping beneath me you'd think a family of bottlenose dolphins or something might leap out of it at any minute. "Why not?" I ask my brother. "Why shouldn't I worry about her? Why shouldn't we both worry about her?"

He doesn't answer at first, and that's fine. I like watching the bubble and roll of the tiny river. Pretty soon, the smack and chatter of players warming up for the next ball game echo across the park. We are surrounded by things that are so alive.

Finally Jeffrey puts his hand on my shoulder. "She's like one of my sliders, Jen. We can't control her. And anyway," he adds, "she just missed another great moment in baseball."

1B *Ron Koertge* **3**

POSITION: FIRST BASE | *ROOKIE YEAR: 1987

*BBI: 10 or so

CAREER HIGHLIGHTS: Writing: *Stoner and Spaz* winning the P.E.N. Award.
Baseball: Going 4-for-4 against AG Econ in a Grad School Game in Tuscon. English Department wins 10–2.

FAVORITE TEAM: The Saint Louis Browns

FAVORITE PLAYER: Eddie Gaedel, the midget whom Bill Veeck sent out to bat against the Tigers in 1951. He had a strike zone of an inch and a half!

BEST GAME EVER: A night game in Triple A / Las Vegas about a decade ago. I don't even remember who played, but it went 16 innings and I was on the edge of my seat.

*Stat key: BBI=Books Batted In (number of books published)
Rookie Year: first book published

RIDING THE PINE: A PLAY

by Ron Koertge

Main Characters:

CHARLIE GARRISON—Team statistician. Twelve years old. Street clothes.

NICK STEVENS—Team member on disabled list. Twelve years old. Left arm in a sling. Wearing Elite Cleaners uniform.

Secondary Characters for Elite Cleaners
(non-speaking parts):

SCOTT DYKSTRA—First base. Nicknamed Scottie.

ANGEL CORDERO—Second base.

JIMMY ESPINOZA—Third base. On his feet a lot.

PHILIP WALCOTT—Shortstop. Nicknamed Philly Cheese.

JEFF KERR—Pitcher. Nicknamed Big Dog.

ANDY WARD—Catcher. Nicknamed Moose. A rah-rah guy.

Doug Lotta—Left field.

Hilton Roark—Center field.

Quentin Jones—Right field. Nicknamed Q. Usually wears his glove on his head.

Off-Stage Voices:

Announcer

Coach for Elite Cleaners team

Coach for Cancun Tanning Salons Team

Time: The present. *Night*

Place: *Community Baseball Field. Dugout at stage level: long bench, long enough to suggest isolation for anyone stage left. Necessary paraphernalia: bats, gloves, chalk, resin, on-deck circle. Stage divided by light. Usually the Elite Cleaners team is in shadow when the focus is on the two boys stage left.*

Act I

<u>At rise:</u> *Lights slowly up on Charlie the statistician, water boy, and general gofer. Beside him is Nick with his arm in a cast. They don't speak until the bench has settled down, giving the audience a chance to get a sense of the other boys, their interest or lack of it in their surroundings.*

Crowd noise is recorded and is used again and again. The usual stuff: a father's gruff encouragement / criticism, isolated clapping, real applause, collective groans. Used appropriately, the repetition should have a ritualistic effect.

It's the bottom of any inning. One out. Off-stage, Jimmy Espinoza is at bat. Angel on deck for Elite Cleaners.

NICK: Jimmy! Focus, baby. Big stick.

(Angel stares out, fiddles with his helmet, getting it just right. Grimaces intently. Puts his body into his practice swings, twisting, maybe, away from some imaginary bean ball. Crack of the bat as Jimmy lines out, then trots onstage, passing Angel on his way to the plate.)

NICK: *(to Charlie)* Those guys always get wood on the ball.

CHARLIE: Which guys?

NICK: Those guys from Mexico.

CHARLIE: Angel's folks are from the Dominican Republic.

NICK: You know what I mean.

(Crack of the bat. Yes! But the elation is short-lived. Groans! Angel trots in from the wings, adjusting the sweat bands at his wrist, something he does almost constantly.)

COACH FOR ELITE: *(voice from off-stage)* You got around on it, Cordero!

(As the Elite Cleaners team gets ready to go on defense, a couple of the guys high-five Angel. Nick stands up and watches his teammates leave the stage to take their positions. He looks where the opposing team's dugout might be.)

NICK: Who's that guy plays short for Cancun?

CHARLIE: Coleman Dewers. Goes to West Hills. Good speed, no glove.

NICK: Coleman. Is that gay enough for you?

CHARLIE: He robbed Angel.

NICK: *(showing his disgust)* Cancun Tanning Salons. How'd you like to have that all over your uniform?

CHARLIE: It's just a sponsor.

ANNOUNCER: Batting for Cancun, third baseman Shelby "Solid Gold" Knox.

NICK: Solid Gold? Why Solid Gold?

CHARLIE: Fort Knox, maybe.

NICK: *(Using his one good hand to cup his mouth, shouts)* Hey Shelby! *(He draws the name out)* Shellll-by. *(Then invention fails him and he sits down. Showing arm-in-sling to Charlie.)* I can't wait to get this thing off.

CHARLIE: What's the doctor say?

NICK: *(looking around)* They might have to do it over.

CHARLIE: You're kidding.

NICK: The X-rays look funny.

CHARLIE: That can't be good.

NICK: I don't get it. Jeff pitches for us, plays Pop Warner football and Gray Y basketball. He's always getting into it with somebody but he never gets hurt.

CHARLIE: My mom says it's better to be lucky than smart. *(As a cheer goes up, he records a strikeout.)* Jeff's got good stuff today.

ANNOUNCER: Now batting, Bruce "The Prowler" Katz.

NICK: I get that one. Cats prowl, right?

CHARLIE: *(nodding as he glances)* There goes Jeff's mom. She comes to every game, then stands in the parking lot half the time.

NICK: Yeah. What's up with that?

CHARLIE: *(matter of fact)* Probably makes her nervous to see him pitch.

NICK: Does your mom come?

CHARLIE: To watch me write stuff down?

NICK: Just, you know, to watch.

CHARLIE: She's working,

NICK: Mine too. Dad never gives her what he's supposed to. She's always taking him to court.

CHARLIE: I saw him the other day.

NICK: In the Mustang?

CHARLIE: Yeah.

NICK: She drops me off at McDonald's, okay? Because she can't stand to see him. On Saturday morning it's like Divorce Central. There's at least six of us in there waiting for our dads. And mine shows up in the new car. The first thing he says is, "How'd you do?" I show him my arm. He says, "Oh, yeah. I forgot." Mom says he's in a coma. Walking around, but in a coma.

(Crack of the bat. Nick watches. Charlie records the out.)

NICK: Good hands, Phil!

CHARLIE: Nobody wins all the time.

NICK: What?

CHARLIE: I was thinking about what your dad asked you, "How'd you do?" And I said, "Nobody wins all the time."

NICK: You can't think like that, man.

CHARLIE: Why not? It's the truth.

NICK: You just can't. If you start thinking you're gonna lose, you're gonna lose.

CHARLIE: So you're saying the guys who win think they're going to win, and the guys who lose think they're going to lose?

NICK: Pretty much. Yeah.

CHARLIE: Statistically unlikely. There's never nine guys thinking the same thing at the same time.

(Crack of the bat. But more that hollow, off-center ping of a dribbling grounder.)

NICK: It's all yours, Scottie! *(He looks at Charlie.)*

Oh, man. Right between his legs. *(After a beat)* All I'm saying is you have to suit up thinking you're . . . *(gropes for a word)*

CHARLIE: Invincible.

NICK: Exactly! Look at Jeff.

CHARLIE: Jeff's lucky.

NICK: *(a little frustrated)* Maybe, but he's got the right attitude. You don't understand 'cause you don't play anymore.

CHARLIE: I don't kid myself. I face facts.

NICK: What facts?

CHARLIE: *(firmly)* That I'm not very good. I've been thinking about making the high school team ever since Pee Wee ball, but I can't even hit what some twelve-year-old is throwing. *If* I made the team, I'd be lucky to get on base one time out of ten. Mostly I'd just let everybody down and ride the pine.

NICK: 'Cause you think like that, see.

CHARLIE: So I should, what—tell myself I'm better than I am?

NICK: Yeah, exactly. And then you will be.

CHARLIE: Is that what you said to your arm?

NICK: *(looking at it)* Huh?

CHARLIE: Did you tell your arm it's gonna be fine? 'Cause if you did, it wasn't listening.

ANNOUNCER: Batting for Cancun, Morgan "White Shoes" Slade.

NICK: *(peering)* They really are white.

(Charlie barely acknowledges Nick. He busies himself with the score sheets.)

NICK: It'd drive me crazy.

CHARLIE: What would?

NICK: Just . . . doing what you do instead of . . . you know.

CHARLIE: Hey, I'll be around the game longer than you will. You just play baseball. I know baseball.

NICK: What's that supposed to mean?

CHARLIE: *(avoiding the subject)* Who's up after Mr. White Shoes?

NICK: *(sarcastically)* Don't ask me. I just play baseball.

CHARLIE: Wolf MacNulty.

NICK: Do you think that's his real name?

CHARLIE: *(shrugs)* The Wolfman owns Jeff. Doug should come in from center to pitch to him because Wolf is batting .127 against southpaws.

NICK: Are you serious?

CHARLIE: *(lifting the stat sheets)* It's all right here. *(Crack of the bat)*

NICK: Hilton! He's going for two! *(Both boys stand and watch.)*

NICK: That guy's got an arm like a noodle.

CHARLIE: That was Doug's ball. Hilton should have just backed him up.

NICK: It's not Hilton's fault. Doug should have called it. He's always got his foot in the bucket.

ANNOUNCER: Batting for Cancun, Wolf "The Wolf-man" MacNulty.

NICK: Look at Quentin. He's not deep enough.

CHARLIE: *(mutters)* Big deal. It's his last game.

NICK: *(absently)* This is summer league, doofus. It's everybody's last game.

CHARLIE: I mean ever.

NICK: You're kidding. Q's good. What's he hitting?

CHARLIE: *(without looking it up)* .312, .313.

NICK: So why's he hanging it up?

CHARLIE: *(shrugs)* Says he wants to concentrate on swimming.

NICK: He's hitting .313 and he wants to concentrate on swimming?

CHARLIE: He said he read this book and got in touch with his inner swimmer.

NICK: Q was reading?

CHARLIE: That's what he says.

NICK: He told you?

CHARLIE: That he had an inner swimmer? Yeah.

NICK: That he was quitting.

CHARLIE: That too.

NICK: I can't believe Q was reading. Q doesn't read. Phil reads.

CHARLIE: No kidding. Phil hides paperbacks in his glove.

NICK: He ought to keep his mind on the game.

CHARLIE: He writes stuff too.

NICK: Get outta town.

CHARLIE: He's working on a new video game like "Grand Theft Auto" but nobody steals anything or gets shot.

NICK: That doesn't sound like any fun.

CHARLIE: I guess his mother got him in touch with his inner censor.

NICK: *(looking out at the field)* Jeff's got the Wolfman two and oh. Still think Doug should be pitching to him?

(Crack of the bat. A solid hit. Charlie leans into his record keeping.)

NICK: *(avoiding the obvious)* You want to know what I think about why Q's quitting?

CHARLIE: Sure.

NICK: It's not swimming. I think he wants to mess with his old man's head. I sure do. I always want to get back at my dad for hurting my mom, and being cheap, and not coming to the hospital when I broke this *(holding up his arm)* and for when we're at McDonald's I tell him I want a double cheese but he'll start hitting on some high school girl and I end up with a fish sandwich. I just don't hate him enough to quit baseball.

CHARLIE: Those are bad.

NICK: What are?

CHARLIE: Those fish sandwiches.

NICK: Tell me about it.

ANNOUNCER: Batting for Cancun, Todd "The Bod" Davis.

NICK: That's a stretch. Get a load of this guy. What does he weigh, ninety-two pounds?

CHARLIE: And ninety-two is about what he's hitting.

NICK: Tod "The Bod." What a stupid nickname.

CHARLIE: Mickey Mantle's was the Commerce Comet.

NICK: That's stupid too. Who called him that?

CHARLIE: Sportswriters, probably.

NICK: Mantle is a great name all by itself.

CHARLIE: Here's a weird one—Whitey Ford was Chairman of the Board, but Richie Ashburn was Whitey.

NICK: It's kind of cool you know all that stuff.

CHARLIE: I guess.

NICK: So do you think I'm right about Q?

CHARLIE: Why he's quitting? Maybe. His old man gets Q out here practicing and they don't stop till it's dark.

NICK: That's not always bad. Jeff's dad does that, and he's cool. But Q's dad never shuts up and nothing Q does is good enough.

CHARLIE: Jeff's mom and Q's dad liked each other once.

NICK: Are you kidding? Who told you?

CHARLIE: My mom was talking on the phone and I kind of listened. Q's dad is the other reason Jeff's mom goes out to the parking lot.

NICK: I thought you said she liked him.

CHARLIE: Did. Doesn't now. Now she hates him.

NICK: Why?

CHARLIE: I don't know. I couldn't hear that part.

NICK: How could she like him?

CHARLIE: Beats me.

NICK: She's got like nine kids.

(A tepid thunk signals Todd "The Bod" Davis's pop-up.)

NICK: Way to go, guys! All we need is three. It's not over till it's over. Plenty of time.

(As his teammates trot back to the bench, Philip and Quentin come in last spaced by a few beats. Nick looks at them both with different eyes. Q sits and puts his glove on his head. Phil settles in, looks around, takes a paperback book out of his pocket, slips it into his mitt, starts to read.)

ANNOUNCER: Philip Walcott should pay more attention to the game.

(Phil is stunned, leaps to his feet. Looks around wildly. Others glance at him curiously. They haven't heard anything. Phil realizes this. Panting, he sits down again. Takes the book out of his glove, wads it up, and throws it in the nearest trash can.)

Curtain / lights out.

Act II

At rise, Nick is pacing and acting anxious. Most of the players are on their feet, rally caps on. There's more trash around.

NICK: We can do this. Andy gets on. Doug brings him home. Q moves Doug up. Walcott homers and we win. We go out winners, okay? Okay? *(to Charlie)* We can do this!

CHARLIE: I heard you.

NICK: You don't think so?

CHARLIE: Phil Walcott has never hit a home run with men on.

NICK: You're negative, man.

CHARLIE: He's not good under pressure.

NICK: My dad's negative, so I know negative.

CHARLIE: I hope Phil comes through. I hope the cover comes off the ball like in that movie *The Natural*. But the numbers say no.

NICK: Screw the numbers. The last couple of innings we've been playing like a team.

CHARLIE: Is that why we're down by three?

NICK: Doesn't matter. There's this little click and it's not nine separate guys anymore. You didn't feel it 'cause you quit, but I felt it. If that second baseman hadn't made that miracle stop, it'd be six—six.

CHARLIE: He's the coach's kid.

NICK: Second base for Cancun?

CHARLIE: Yeah. Bob Hickok.

NICK: Wild Bob Hickok.

CHARLIE: The Wildman. He's really good. Everybody in his family is. His sister pitches and she's got real heat.

NICK: You watch girls' slow-pitch?

CHARLIE: Sometimes. I might like to scout. You know—be one. Move around a lot. Find guys nobody's ever heard of. It's like a treasure hunt.

NICK: You might not be home for your birthday or Christmas.

CHARLIE: So?

(Andy comes off the bench. Everyone is on their feet. Nick angles away from the seated Charlie, joins the others in encouraging Andy.)

ANNOUNCER: Batting for Elite Cleaners, Andrew "Moose" Ward.

(Mooing sounds from Ward's teammates. Nick drifts back toward Charlie, but still with his eye on the plate.)

CHARLIE: Look at Scott.

NICK: So?

CHARLIE: He hates Andy.

NICK: He doesn't hate Andy.

CHARLIE: Yeah, he does. Watch him.

NICK: What? *(He looks, sees, frowns.)* He's like everybody else.

CHARLIE: No way. He's not clapping. He's not yelling as loud.

NICK: He doesn't hate Andy.

CHARLIE: Okay.

NICK: Why would he?

CHARLIE: He wanted to be called Moose. He doesn't like Scottie. Scottie is a dog.

NICK: Who calls him Scottie?

CHARLIE: Moose.

NICK: *(to batter)* Take your time, baby. Good eye.

CHARLIE: Scott says the only good thing about losing is that Moose loses too.

NICK: How do you know this stuff?

CHARLIE: Guys talk. They stand around *(nods toward the Gatorade cooler)* and talk. I hear. I'm kind of invisible. Or they just tell me because they think I don't count.

(Crack of the bat)

NICK: Yes. No. Yes!

(Groans followed immediately by cheers)

NICK: Mr. All-League Big Shot Wild Bob Hickok muffed that one.

COACH FOR CANCUN: *(faint but harsh)* Are you thinking of the pizza you're gonna get after the game, Bobby? Well, you're not getting a pizza after the game. Everybody else is, but not you. You're gonna sit in the car and think about how you ruined things for everybody.

CHARLIE: *(pointing)* I hate that guy.

NICK: That's Hickok's dad, right?

CHARLIE: The coach, yeah. And Hickok has to ride home with that and listen to it at dinner.

NICK: And I thought my old man was bad.

CHARLIE: *(head shake)* He's nothing compared to this guy.

NICK: What a jerk.

CHARLIE: How can Hickok stand having his dad rag on him all the time: "Get your head in the game!" "Sacrifice your body." "Take one for the team." Some kids just crack, you know? They break. There's like eight-year-olds with ulcers because they can't turn a double play.

NICK: Is that what happened to you?

CHARLIE: *(after a beat or two)* I didn't get an ulcer exactly.

NICK: My dad says if it doesn't kill you, it makes you stronger.

CHARLIE: Does that come with the fish sandwich?

(Crack of the bat. Nick is on his feet.)

NICK. Yes. Oh, yes. Way to go, Doug! Stand-up double. Six to four. Man on and nobody out!

CHARLIE: *(writes it down)* Nice.

NICK: Nice? Is that all you can say?

CHARLIE: I don't mean just the two-bagger. I mean things worked out. Nice that way.

NICK: They didn't just work out. Doug killed that slider.

CHARLIE: That wasn't a slider. That was a mistake. Nobody on Cancun throws sliders. They're all fast-ball, changeup, fastball. What was sweet was when Hickock's dad ran on the field and lost his mind at his kid. Now everybody's thinking, "Oh, man. If I screw up, I'm next." Talk about not having your head in the game.

NICK: But Doug was ready, okay. He was positive. He wasn't thinking "Nobody wins all the time."

CHARLIE: Maybe.

NICK: *(to batter)* Q! Nice easy stoke. Bring Dougie home.

CHARLIE: He doesn't like to be called Dougie.

NICK: His e-mail is Dougie dot com.

CHARLIE: E-mail is different than out loud.

NICK: Doug! Wake up, man. *(To Charlie)* Look at him! He's glued to the base!

CHARLIE: Probably doesn't want to get picked off.

NICK: No kidding. He can strike out five times in a row and shake it off. But he gets caught leaning once and he just about cries.

CHARLIE: I never stole a base in my life.

NICK: *(after a beat)* We used to e-mail and stuff.

CHARLIE: You and Dougie dot com?

NICK: Yeah. Just, you know: who had the short skirt

on at school. Who's going with who and would it last all day. Then I got hurt and nada.

CHARLIE: He's probably afraid if it happened to you, it could happen to him.

NICK: Getting hurt?

CHARLIE: Yeah. He's totally superstitious. He's got a magic crystal and a rabbit's foot.

NICK: Well, he sure stopped writing when I went in the hospital.

CHARLIE: I rest my case.

NICK: *(looking at his arm)* I took number thirteen on purpose.

CHARLIE: It's a good number.

NICK: Big Dog just about cried, he wanted seven so bad.

CHARLIE: You know who was cool was Doug and Jimmy. They were like "whatever." Remember that big deal about numbers?

NICK: They're not magic. Just because you've got A-Rod's number, no way are you A-Rod. You used to have eleven, didn't you?

CHARLIE: Yeah.

NICK: Eleven's a pretty good number.

(Crack of the bat)

NICK: Ouch. Oh, man. Their shortstop is down.

(All the players stand. Charlie too, but only after he writes a couple of things.)

NICK: Do you see blood?

CHARLIE: Not from here. First baseman for Acres of Books bled all over the place last week. Took one in the nose.

NICK: Six to five. Man on second. We got all the momentum.

CHARLIE: He's not getting up.

NICK: And nobody out.

CHARLIE: He sort of is.

NICK: Everybody'll clap.

CHARLIE: Not too much. Remember him, first time at bat? Pointing to the fence, running his mouth? People hate that.

(Tepid applause. Nick applauds too, but halfheartedly.)

NICK: He just got the wind knocked out of him.

CHARLIE: Like he's going to grab his jock with everybody watching.

NICK: I told my mom if I ever get hurt, do not run on the field. I'm wearing a uniform, for godsake, I'm like a warrior and then something happens and all of a sudden my mom is there with a Kleenex.

CHARLIE: When I played left, I always backed up. I always wanted it to bounce before it got to me.

NICK: That's the way you do it. You play the ball. Sometimes—

CHARLIE: *(interrupting)* I *always* backed up.

NICK: *(embarrassed a little, talks it up for the next batter)* Walcott. Up to you, my man. One swing of the bat and we're golden. We got all the momentum, baby. All of it. *(Settles back down, glancing around.)* Who are those girls, Charlie?

CHARLIE: Jeff's big sister is the middle one. And her friends, I guess.

NICK: Man, his whole family shows up. That guy with the cowbell is his grandpa.

CHARLIE: You won't remember this, but we were all at the zoo like on a field trip or something, and a bunch of us went to pee, which was kind of a big deal because we were like seven or eight and Mrs. Arnold couldn't come in with us, and there wasn't a man teacher around, so she sent us all in together in case there was some perv in there, in which case we should all run out together.

NICK: I was in on this?

CHARLIE: I said you wouldn't remember. But what I'm saying is we're in there and we're all half goofy because we're on our own and there are these grown-ups we don't know taking leaks and those warm air things you punch instead of towels, and these kids from our class, Ronnie Van Walleghen and Lester Chang, were like, "Jeff, Jeff, look at this," and "Jeff, over here," and "Jeff, are you ready to go?" And I thought, he's the one.

NICK: The one what?

CHARLIE: The One. He's like eight and he's popular. Nobody was saying, "Charlie, Charlie," or "Nick, Nick."

NICK: I don't think I was there.

CHARLIE: Yeah, you were.

Nick: *(as Phil walks into the wings)* What's Coach want with Walcott?

Charlie: It's just a psych job. Their pitcher's so nervous, he's already chewing his glove. Coach wants him to eat the whole thing.

Nick: So I was there, but Jeff was the one?

Charlie: At the zoo? Yeah.

Nick: How does that happen?

Charlie: I don't know.

Nick: I'd like to be the one. For a while, anyway.

Charlie: Who wouldn't.

Nick: I hate it when girls watch me bat.

Charlie: I hate it when anybody watches me bat.

Nick: It's worse with girls. I always end up looking at strike three.

Charlie: Jeff is so cool, if that happens to him he just shrugs, and they like him more.

Nick: *(turning his attention to the game)* Here we go! Big stick, Phil baby. You own this guy. *(To Charlie)* What's Cancun gonna throw?

Charlie: *(shrugs)* Who knows. That pitcher just wants this over with. Can't you almost hear him, "God, let me get this guy out and I'll never ask you for anything."

Nick: Not gonna happen. Phil, make him pitch to you, baby.

Charlie: He should just get some wood on the ball. I told you he never hit a home run in . . .

(Crack of the bat)

NICK: Oh, my God. It's gone. Charlie, look at it go!

(The bench erupts. But with no sound and almost in slow motion. They congratulate each other, wave their hats, and celebrate. But it's like it's all happening underwater. Then they pour off stage to greet their hero. Charlie sits alone, makes one last notation on the pages in his lap, sets those aside, and gets up.)

There is some debris lying around, mostly crushed paper cups and some equipment. He puts the latter in a large canvas bag and drops the trash in a nearby receptacle. Picking up a bat, he walks toward the apron of the stage, looks out, and points toward the balcony.

Charlie takes his stance, cocks the bat, narrows his eyes, steps into an imaginary fastball, and swings for the fences. He watches the invisible ball disappear, blithely tosses the bat aside, and tips his hat as he jogs toward the sound, now audible, of the team celebrating.

CURTAIN

OF **David Rice** **8**

POSITION: CENTER FIELD | *ROOKIE YEAR: 1992

*BBI: 2

ROOKIE YEAR: 1992. *Persona*. A university journal. And then the same year in *Bilingual Review*.

FAVORITE TEAM: The Grasshoppers. My mother's softball team in the Rio Grande Valley.

FAVORITE PLAYER: My mom is my favorite player. She was the pitcher for the Grasshoppers.

BEST GAME EVER: Any game is great as long as they serve nachos. That's what I think.

TOMBOY FORGIVENESS

by David Rice

"Get ready, 'cause this is gonna knock you over," Tía Bertha said with a sly grin as she leaned over the pitching mound with the eager softball in her hand. Our mother, standing firm over home plate, swirled her bat and spit. "You can't strike me out," she said. When my sister, Rosanna, and I saw Mom spit, we knew she was going to hit the ball with all her strength, so we backed up. Bertha adjusted her baseball cap, kicked some dirt off the pitching mound, and spun her arm in a blur, and the ball shot out like a cannonball. In one quick move Mom pulled and swung the bat at full speed and slammed the ball in our direction. "I got it," Rosanna shouted, and the ball smacked her glove. She raised the ball in the air. "It's still hot." Mom adjusted her cap. "Think I'm ready for the tournament this weekend?" she said with a wide smile. Bertha let out a booming laugh and kicked dirt off the pitching mound like a bull ready to charge. "Girl, you and me. In the final," she said.

Bertha was our mom's best friend, even though they played softball against each other with every fiber in their being. We called Bertha Tía Bertha because we saw her so much, and she was also our mother's hairdresser and made sure our mom was the only Mexican American woman in town with bright blond hair or cherry red hair. Every three months Mom walked into the house with a new color and a new attitude. "Keep them guessing," she'd say, and she was the same way in softball.

You never knew what she was going to do. Line drive, bunt, grounder, or hit a home run. But you weren't going to be ready. Our father said the same about her. *"Ésta mujer,"* he'd say in frustration, but every year his brake shop sponsored Mom's softball team with new uniforms and equipment. The only catch was, he liked to be third-base coach, and he was good at yelling and swinging his arms like a deranged monkey. At every game he'd shout orders like a bully. The softball team lasted longer than their marriage.

When we were little, Mom and Dad were always fighting, and then all of a sudden he found a new wife, and a new family. We knew the brand-new sons because they were our age and we saw them at school all the time. It was something we got used to, and by the time we got to junior high, everybody knew the story, so it didn't bother us too much. When our parents divorced it was Bertha who was by our mother's side through the whole ordeal, and she did her best to cheer Mom up.

Our hometown of Edcouch hosted the softball tournament, and teams from Elsa, La Villa, Monte Alto, La Blanca, Hargill, Santa Rosa, and Weslaco filled our ballpark. Edcouch only had 2,656 people, but during the tournament, our town doubled in size.

Every year Mom and Tía Bertha were the rock stars of the tournament and people shook their hands as they walked by. Mom was best hitter in the league, and Tía Bertha, the best pitcher. When Beto's Brake Shop played against Bertha's Beauty Shop, the bleachers would get packed with fans cheering for both teams. There were no losers.

One week before the tournament, the Ruben pony express broke down, and Rosanna got some messed-up news. Rosanna was in eighth grade, and she had a class with Ruben, our dad's stepson. They got along okay, but Mom used Ruben as a post office. If Mom wanted to send a message to Dad, she'd write it down on a piece of paper and seal it in an envelope and give it to Rosanna, and Rosanna would give it to Ruben, and Ruben gave it to Dad. It wasn't very mature, but the postage was free.

I was walking down the school halls between classes when Rosanna came barreling toward me, brushing kids aside like a hurricane with the latest news. She took my arm and pushed me against the wall.

"Guess what Ruben just told me?" she said, like it was the most important thing she ever heard.

I jerked my arm from her grasp. "What, that he wets the bed?"

"Pffff. *Grosero*." Then in a secret hush, she said, "He told me that Dad is seeing some other woman."

"What?" I said.

"Yeah, Ruben said that his mom kicked Dad out of the house," Rosanna said.

"Ah man, are you serious?" I said with a chuckle, 'cause I thought it was kinda funny.

"Yeah, and you'll never guess who Dad is seeing."

I shrugged my shoulders. "Who?"

Rosanna took a deep breath and shook her head in disbelief. "Tía Bertha."

You know how in cartoons when someone gets hit on the head with a frying pan and their head vibrates, making ringing sounds? That's what I felt like when my sister told me that Dad was seeing Tía Bertha.

"What?" I grabbed my sister's arms to keep my head from shaking to pieces.

"I know, I know. It's so messed up," she said.

"Does Mom know?" I said.

"I don't know."

"What are we going to do?" I said.

My sister let out a sigh. "Poor Mom," she said.

The rest of the day I walked in a daze, turning over the possibilities of Mom's reaction. Even though my parents were divorced and all, it was still uncool what Tía Bertha was doing, but at the same time it wasn't any of my business. That afternoon my sister and I walked home together, something we didn't do often, but we needed each other. It was Monday night softball practice, and we thought that probably one of Mom's teammates would tell her the news. When we got home, we decided to clean up the house real nice so if Mom came home in a bad mood, at least the house was clean. By 5:30 Mom wasn't home yet, and we called her cell phone, but she didn't answer.

"Do you think Mom knows?" I asked my sister.

Rosanna threw her arms up. "By now the whole town knows," she said

It was close to 10:00 when Mom walked in the house.

We were watching TV and we stood up. She was wearing her softball practice clothes, and she was covered in sweat. I don't remember my parents' divorce, but what I was feeling must have been what I felt when our father left us. Mom wears her emotions like a jacket. Everyone can see what she's thinking.

"Mom, you okay?" my sister asked.

"You guys heard, huh?"

We nodded.

"I ran four miles after practice. You know how it is. You just gotta sweat it out." She pulled her head back and exhaled. Then she brought her head down and shook it like boxers do before a fight. "I'm just going to stay focused on the tournament."

The next day a few of her teammates came to the house to go over the batting order. Mom's softball friends were loud and loved to drink beer out of bottles as they decided who would hit singles, doubles, and home runs. Tía Bertha was usually there to help out with the list since she knew the batting styles of every player, but not this time. Her name wasn't even mentioned, and her laugh didn't fill our house. All week long there was this dark cloud hanging over Mom. I had never seen her look so sad, and I knew that the tournament was going to be make or break for her.

Saturday morning was gloomy, and there were low

dark clouds as far as you could see. Mom had her game face on, and so did my sister. Rosanna was the bat girl and equipment manager, and took her jobs seriously. My job was to mix Gatorade in a big cooler with lots of ice, and stay out of their way as we loaded Mom's truck. I rode in the back of the truck surrounded by mesh nylon bags of gear for the short drive to the City of Edcouch Ball Park. Four fields of hard-hitting softball action. The tournament was fast. Only eight teams with four fields and double elimination, and each game with a time limit of one hour and fifteen minutes.

When we parked, Mom's teammates walked up with the game schedule. The first team they would play was Bertha's Beauty Shop. Mom nodded. "Well then, they will be the first team to lose." When both teams stood in line on the field for the "Star-Spangled Banner," you could feel the frustration between the teams. It was strange because the players were all friends and many of them had grown up together, but they didn't know how to act. Fans were at a loss too, but secretly they were taking sides. But in the end, everyone knew the game would have the answers.

Our father stayed away from Mom, and Bertha stayed away from our father. My sister and I said very little, and cheering for Beto's Brake Shop didn't feel right because we felt like we were cheering for our father, since his name was on their uniforms. The game started off with Bertha pitching the first strike-out of the day. You could see Bertha taking the game seriously and doing her best, but she couldn't strike out Mom.

Each time Mom was up to bat, she got on base. With four minutes left in the game, Bertha's Beauty Shop was up by one. Our father made short paces behind third base, clapping his hands. "Come on, the clock is ticking." Mom's team had one runner on second, and our mother was up to bat. Mom picked up some dirt and rubbed her hands. Bertha adjusted her cap and put the ball right down the middle. "Strike one," the umpire shouted. Mom took a step back and moved her head side to side and then returned to the batter's box with the bat pulled back tight. Bertha pitched a blur, and the umpire shouted, "Strike two." Mom took a step back and gave her bat a couple of short swings and then got ready for Bertha's third pitch. Bertha threw low, but this time Mom's bat was there to say hello and good-bye.

The ball sailed deep into right field, and the woman on second scrambled home. Mom sprinted through first and rounded second before the outfielder threw the ball in. Our father was shouting, "Go,go,go. Take it home." My sister and I were standing, shouting the same thing along with the crowd. Mom blew through third, and Bertha caught the ball and threw it hard to home. As the ball touched the catcher's glove, Mom slammed her and the ball shot out of the glove. "Safe!" the umpire shouted with one minute left on the clock as Mom and the catcher hit the ground. There was a roar of cheers from the stands. Bertha's Beauty Shop advanced to the loser's bracket, and Beto's Brake Shop advanced to the winner's bracket.

By noon, my sister and I had sore throats from all the yelling and shouting. Mom's team couldn't make a mistake if they tried. Meanwhile Bertha's team was on a winning streak in the loser's bracket. Talk throughout the tournament was about a final game between Beto's Brake Shop and Bertha's Beauty Shop, and each game moved Mom and Bertha closer. Mom's team cut Juanita's Flower Shop to pieces, and Bertha's team burned down The Hot Tamale House. Usually the teams who lost would leave, but everyone knew that the final game was more than just a game, and lots of people got on their cell phones, and even more people showed up.

My sister told me that people were betting to see who would win the tournament, and some were even betting that our mom and Tía Bertha would get into a fistfight.

"What?" I said.

"You know that Mom and Tía Berta can be big tomboys," my sister said with a worried look. "We need to talk to Mom."

Five minutes before the final game, we told Mom about the bets going around.

Mom smacked her fist into her glove. "I'll bet your father started those stupid bets."

"But Mom, you're not going to get into a fight with Tía Bertha, are you?" my sister asked.

Mom looked shocked. "Bertha is my best friend. I would never hurt her."

"But you're not talking to her. And all your friends are mad at her," I said.

"But I'm not mad at her," Mom said. "I'm just hurt." She could see we were worried. "Hey, it's going to be okay. I'm not going to let your father ruin this too. Just cheer for Bertha like you cheer for me, and everything will be fine." We gave each other a group hug and Mom darted to her team.

In the stands, fans were stacked like people watermelons and they were standing all over the place in the 100-degree heat, but it was worth it. Within thirty minutes of play, Bertha's team was up by two, and my mom's team was struggling to get a grip on the game. One hour into the final Mom and Bertha squared off again, but Bertha was too hot to stop, and in three fast pitches, Mom was out. When Bertha's team was up to bat, Mom's team didn't let one player past first base.

There were only seven minutes left in the game when Mom's team came up to bat. They were down by two, but you could feel something was going to happen. The first batter, Virna, knocked the first pitch into left field, and made it to first base. The second batter, our mom, walked to home plate with a wall of cheers behind her. Bertha stayed focused and burned the first pitch. Strike! Mom stepped back and regained her thoughts and raised her bat for the second pitch. Bertha's second pitch was faster. "Strike two!" the umpire shouted. The fans went nuts with whistles and shouts.

Mom stepped back from the plate, adjusted her cap, got in the batter's box, and pointed to left field. The crowd let out an "Ooooooooo." Bertha took in a deep breath and fired another rocket, but this time Mom exploded the ball as promised. The crowd went crazy. Mom reached second base, and Virna advanced to third base. You could see our father already giving orders to Virna about getting home.

Two minutes were left in the game, and the third batter, Delia, was always worth a hit. Bertha tightened up and then threw like lightning, but Delia's bat was already in motion, and in a flash the ball went right back at Bertha. The crowd let out a gasp as the ball hit Bertha right in the face. Bertha let out a loud cry, and the way she went down, you could tell she was hurt. Our father started shouting at Virna to run, and Virna made it home. Our mom ran through third and then slowed down and looked back at Bertha and then ran to Bertha. Our father went nuts, shouting, "What are you doing? Forget her!"

Then Mom knelt by Bertha and helped her sit up, but our father kept shouting. The crowd fell silent, and all you could hear was our father screaming insults at our mother. Mom looked at our father, who was stomping and kicking dirt like a spoiled kid. Then she looked at us. We were in the dugout, and both of us were clutching the steel fence. My sister's eyes began to water, and she turned to me and took my hand, and we nodded at Mom. We could see tears rolling down Mom's face, and she smiled at us. She slowly reached for the ball, and our father went ape crazy and starting screaming, "Don't you dare touch that ball! Leave it alone."

Our mom put her hand on the ball, clenched it, and picked it up. She raised it above her head for the world to see, and everyone held their breath. Then there was a break in the dark clouds, and a ray of light embraced Tía Bertha and Mom. And then Mom turned her hand and let the ball drop into the red dirt. The fans let out a sea of cheers that poured on the field and lifted Tía Bertha and our mother. I looked at Rosanna, and she turned to me and said softly, "Mom is the best," and it echoed through every ballpark in the world.

C **2**

Maria Testa

POSITION: CATCHER | *ROOKIE YEAR: 1994

*BBI: 8

CAREER HIGHLIGHTS: Graduating from Yale Law School and deciding I'd really rather be a writer. Everything's been one big highlight since then.

FAVORITE TEAM: New York Yankees

FAVORITE PLAYER: Derek Jeter and Mariano Rivera

BEST GAME EVER: 1978 American League East division playoff game (the Bucky Dent game).

SMILE LIKE JETER

by Maria Testa

HARMONY *(or, Why My Father Noticed Derek Jeter)*

Watch him, son
my father said from the beginning,
before we moved to Maine,
before I was even old enough
for T-ball.
I don't know much about baseball,
but I don't think
everyone
looks like that
when they play shortstop . . .

So I turned to the television
and watched number 2
with pinstripes
for the very first time:
Ground ball
deep in the hole
he turns
he leaps
he throws . . .
. . . he smiles.

My father smiled, too.

There's something about the way he plays
that makes me think
of harmony.

TALENT

I could always catch.

My mother says she saw talent early on
but she didn't know exactly
what to call it
at the time.
When I was a little kid

I would throw my alphabet blocks
up to the ceiling
just so I could catch them
on the way down.
My hands and feet
were always bare
even in winter
because mittens and socks
were so much fun to toss up high
and so easy to catch
before they hit the ground.
It didn't take long
for me to discover
fuzzy yellow tennis balls
and the side of the house,
and after that,
a sense of rhythm
steady and strong,
almost a second heartbeat.

My father would stand outside
and watch sometimes,
shaking his head
as if he liked what he saw.

I don't know much about baseball,
but I don't think
everyone

looks like that
when they throw a ball
against the side of a house . . .

WELL-ROUNDED

In the meantime,
I learned to play the violin.

There's nothing incredible about this,
and I'm a better-than-okay
not amazing player,
good for my age
but not that good.
My father plays the violin too,
and so did his father
and so have generations
of D'Amico men, who,
my mother says,
have always sought
perfect harmony
in their music
if not
in their lives.

AND THEN WE MOVED TO MAINE

For the first twelve years
of my life
my father was a part-time
laborer
and a rest-of-the-time
violinist,
taking it upon himself
to make sure I joined him
for an hour every day.
Even a shortstop
needs some music
in his life.

"I love music
and baseball
as much as anyone,"
my mother would say,
"but somebody's got
to go to work
around here."

So we moved to Maine,
way up the coast to nowhere
where they needed nurses
and a part-time fisherman
was a fine thing to be

and there's maybe
one good month
for playing baseball.

FOUR-BY-FOUR

I showed up
on the first day of Little League
in Nowhere, Maine,
expecting a tryout,
some kind of chance
to show what I could do.

"The answer to my prayers!"
one man proclaimed,
planting himself in front of me
clutching a clipboard
and looking just a little
too happy.
"A perfect square,
four-by-four,
the perfect body,
a catcher made in heaven."

"I'm a shortstop," I said

so loudly
that I didn't quite believe it
myself.
"Not anymore,"
my new coach said,
throwing his arm across my shoulders
and pointing to some kids
tossing a ball around the infield.
"That's a shortstop."

I looked.

It wasn't hard
to figure out
just who I was supposed to be
looking at.

Long arms,
long legs
turning
leaping
throwing . . .
. . . smiling . . .
and long black hair
tied back tight
with a bright blue ribbon,
shiny black hair

swinging back and forth
gracefully.
Coach stuck out his hand.

"Welcome to East Shore,
Mr. Four-by-Four.
You're my new catcher."

WHAT I TOLD MY FATHER

I watched my father practice
that night,
staring at his hands
like I had never seen them
before.

My hands are like my father's,
short, thick fingers,
square, wide palms,
the hands of a catcher
made for a mitt,
yet somehow, my father's hands
fly across the strings
up and down the violin
not exactly gracefully
but close.

"I have your hands,"
I said out loud
as I silently wondered
if anyone had ever
called my father
Mr. Five-by-Five.

My father did not know
what I was talking about,
but I knew that he thought
he did.

The violin is in our blood
but not in our bodies.
Not in our hands
but in our hearts.

"I'm the catcher
on my new baseball team," I said.
"The coach thinks it's in my body."

THE SHORTSTOP'S NAME IS RUTH

She nodded at me
when I chose number 2,
nodded like she was granting me

some kind of permission.
Everybody seemed to know
that the shortstop would be number 3,
like the Babe's name and number
were both hers
by some sort of birthright.
I grabbed my number 2 jersey
and headed over to the plate
for my first lesson
in my new identity.

"Welcome home, Mr. Four-by-Four,"
Coach greeted me.
"I'm expecting great things
from you."

THE TOOLS OF IGNORANCE

"They call them
the tools of ignorance, you know,"
Ruth said,
as she stood there
watching me struggle
and fumble
and just about give up
trying to strap on

shin guards
and a chest protector.

I didn't even want
to look at her,
but I could tell she was trying
not to smile.

"Want some help?" she asked.

I didn't really mean
to growl
or snarl
or sound quite so ignorant,
but I just couldn't seem
to help myself.

"What I want," I said
in a voice not my own,
"is to play shortstop."

MY FATHER TALKS MUSIC
(because he doesn't know much about baseball . . .)

It's all about harmony,
my father said.

A melody
can be just fine on its own,
but the perfect harmony
completes the sound,
fills in the gaps,
and the result . . .
is music.

I tightened my bow,
placed it on the strings,
and told my father
I was ready to play.

UNDERSTANDING THE MASK

No one knows what you're thinking
when you wear
a catcher's mask.

This, I decided, was a good thing.

No one knew
how much time I spent
crouched behind the plate
looking around the batter,
looking past the pitcher,

looking right at the shortstop.
No one knew
how many innings I spent
imagining I was filling the hole
between second and third,
wearing my number 2
for all the world to see.
No one knew
how jealous I was.

And no one knew
that the way
Ruth played shortstop
made me think
of harmony.

FRIENDS *(Sort of)*

I almost apologized.

I was standing next to Ruth
outside the batting cage
at the time.

"I've worn number 2
all my life," I said,

my words coming
from nowhere.

Ruth nodded.
"I sort of figured
that one out
all by myself," she said.

"So. That's why," I said.

"Got it," she said.

It seemed to be enough.

LONG BALL

So Coach was right after all.

It didn't take long
for me to become
a pretty good catcher.
The perfect square
turned out to be a natural
at blocking the plate,
knocking down wild pitches,

and gunning out runners
at second base.

"I am one smart guy," Coach said.

But no one expected
the long ball.

I started connecting
at the plate,
driving the ball high and deep
and out of here
so often that Ruth led the team
in chants of
Four! Four! Four-by-Four!
every time I stepped up
to the plate.

"I must be a genius," Coach said.

RUTH, IN MY FACE *(and All in One Breath)*

You're good, you know,
you can think on your feet
and you're fast for a catcher, too.

You could be
a really good ballplayer,
just like your number 2
but only if
you really want to be,
only if
you really love baseball.
Do you love baseball?
Because if you do,
before you even think about
hitting like Jeter
running like Jeter
or throwing like Jeter,
you're going to have
to learn
to smile like Jeter.

LIKE AN ARTIST

And then,
it was Coach's turn.

"There's something different
going on with you,
different from the other players,
different from what I expected.

Tell me, Mr. Four-by-Four,
what else do you do?
What else do you love?
What else makes you who you are?"
"I play the violin," I said
before the words
had even formed in my mind,
and surprising myself
when I continued:
"I love to play
the violin,
just like my father."

I stared right at Coach,
daring him to laugh,
daring him to turn my words
into some kind of joke.

Coach smiled and nodded
and stared right back at me.
"It makes sense," he said simply.
"You play baseball
like someone who sees things
a little differently.
You play baseball
like an artist."

ALL-STAR

"I'm an All-Star," I told my father.
"Only two players
were chosen from my team,
me and Ruth.
Ruth and me,
All-Stars."

My father looked at me
and liked what he saw.
He hugged me tight
and messed up my hair.

*Is this Ruth as happy
as you are?*

I thought for a moment
and nodded.
"It's all about harmony,"
I said, because I knew
it was true.

OWNING IT

I show up
at the first All-Star practice,
and Ruth runs across the field
to meet me,
tossing a jersey
into my catcher's hands.
"I saved it for you," she says,
proud as can be,
and I hold up number 2.
"Thanks," I say,
"but I think this time
I'll take number 4."
Ruth shakes her head, surprised.
"For who?" she asks. "Lou Gehrig?"
"No," I answer. "For me."
Ruth's eyes widen
in amazement,
and then she laughs out loud.
"I do love baseball, you know,"
I say, and before the words
are out of my mouth
I am running toward the infield
with Ruth by my side
running and smiling,
just like me.

P | John H. Ritter | 1

POSITION: PITCHER | *ROOKIE YEAR: 1998

*BBI: 4

ROOKIE YEAR: Books: 1998, Short stories: 1994 in *Spitball: The Baseball Literary Magazine.*

CAREER HIGHLIGHTS: Winning the 1999 International Reading Association's YA Book Award for my first novel, *Choosing Up Sides.*

FAVORITE TEAM: San Diego Padres

FAVORITE PLAYER: Currently: Khalil Greene, a.k.a. "Jeff Spicoli," Shortstop, San Diego Padres. All-time favorite: Dizzy Dean, Pitcher, St. Louis Cardinals, 1930s.

BEST GAME EVER: Toss-up. Our final game during my sophomore year in high school, we won the league pennant, and I won the team MVP award, hitting .545 over the last half of the season. But years later, over the course of a double-header I went 7 for 9 at the plate, including my only 5 for 5 day ever (in the first game).

BASEBALL CRAZY

by *John H. Ritter*

"Sometimes people ask me, 'Hey, man, was Cruz de la Cruz based on a real guy?' And sometimes I say yes."

Let me tell you a little story about Frankie Alvarez, the finest secret agent baseball player I've ever known. I first met Frankie in the summer of 1963 on a rocky, red-dirt baseball diamond behind the Granite Hills High School gym. It was our first day on a brand-new team in a part of town where there'd never been an organized baseball league before. We were eleven years old and we were baseball crazy.

Our manager back then was old Mr. Hansen. Nice guy. Quiet, small-town plumber who drove a duct-tape-gray pickup truck. My dad was the coach, and on that day he stood at home plate hitting flies and grounders to half the team while the other half ran the bases. And it didn't take any one of us too long to see that Frankie Alvarez was a grandstand of a baseball man and a rocket in cleats. Fast? He could go from stock-still to full speed in two steps, circle the bases in a barn-fire frenzy, and cross home plate ready to dance.

Seemed like to him, it was either illegal, immoral, or outright mortifying to spy an open base up ahead. If he was on first, second base was coming right up, and third was in immediate danger.

"How'd you get so fast?" Mr. Hansen asked him.

Even though it was a dumb question, the rest of us waiting to run moved a step closer, in case there really was some secret way we could learn to blow around the bases like a Santa Ana wind.

Frankie looks up at him with one eyebrow cocked and aims a finger toward the clouds as if he were about to beam out a beacon of ancient truth. "Easy," he says. "Every morning before breakfast, I drink a long, tall bottle of hot sauce." Then, on the next hit, he tears off running again.

None of us say a word. We're fixed on Frankie's flying feet, watching as he turns a little infield chopper into a single on pure hustle.

"Atta batta!" Mr. Hansen yells. "Hey, out there. Whatsa matta? Let's talk it up. Let's hear some *chatta*!"

Now that was pretty embarrassing, to be honest. Mr. Hansen's corny baseball "chatta" was a little extra cheerleading we didn't really want or need. But his son, Jeffrey, was a nice guy, so we let all that slide, even muttering an "Atta way, Frank-ay!" or two ourselves.

Now Frankie's standing on first. My dad hits a lazy fly ball to centerfield and what does Frankie do? He tags up and skedaddles down to second like a rabbit crossing a blacktop road in the middle of July.

The shortstop—I forget who it was—he runs over to cover second base, screaming, "Throw it here! Throw it to second!" Garrett, in center, flips the ball out of his mitt, steps up, and fires.

But Frankie never even saw the throw. I mean, how could he, with his back turned? What I'm saying is, he was already rounding second and pounding down the path to third before the ball had flown halfway to the infield.

Second sacker, he cuts it off and was about to wing it to the shortstop, but the guy waves him off, screaming, "No, third base! Three, three!"

And the same thing. The ball gets to third all right, but by then Frankie was already hotfooting it on home. It was unbelievable. He had tagged up and *scored* all the way from first base on a routine, everyday fly ball to center. No one'd ever seen anything like it. Not even an old baseball man like my dad.

When it's time for our group to take the field, I notice

Frankie running out wearing a toy glove. At first, I think this is another one of his jokes. I mean, he's playing second base, and his glove is nothing more than some sort of a gray-green plastic thing you'd buy off a rack at the grocery store. Not much bigger than his own hand.

Then right away, my dad whacks a sharp grounder to second base. It hits a loose rock and takes a bad hop, but Frankie stays right with it. He scoops it up against his chest and makes a quick, side-arm flick to first, smack dab on the *peso*. I could tell by the serious gleam in his eyes, the glove was no joke. It was all he had and it was majestic.

After I saw all that, I liked him even more. Because what I really saw standing there was a gutsy, dirt-lot poor boy, just like me, who could flat-out play some ball. On pure instinct. "Baseball born and baseball raised," my dad called it. But I called it "baseball crazy."

By the end of practice, we were all pretty bedazzled. When Mr. Hansen passed out our new uniforms, Frankie took his jersey and shook it open, holding the huge white shirt up to his skinny chest. The sheen on the maroon-striped sleeves sparkled in the sun. "I'm sleeping in this tonight," he declared. Silently, eleven other guys decided they were going to do the same thing.

Then he folds the brim of his new cap into a peak, like the ridge of a roof, but before he puts it on, he pauses.

You see, back then, those were Elvis days, soon to be Beatle days, but were still Brylcreem hair gunk "A little dab'll do ya" days, and a few of us, me and Frankie included, wore our hair like the ballplayers in the TV commercials—all slicked back and tricked to attract.

So just before Frankie lowers his hat to his head, he says, "You guys wanna know why my hair's so slick and sleek?"

He doesn't even wait for an answer. Just sets his cap down easy, like a jaybird landing on a fencepost, and says, "Bacon grease." We all spin away, hooting and whapping our hats at him, but he just laughs and says, "Yep. A little slab'll do ya."

Over the first half of the season, Frankie built quite a reputation for himself, on and off the baseball diamond, for being dizzy and daring and really good at whatever he did, whether it was playing ball or playing secret agent James Bond, double-O seven, ladies' man.

However, one thing really bugged him. Bugged us all.

There was one particular team in our league—the Coyotes—that we could never beat. They were managed by a cop we called "Mr. Clean." His real name was Cartridge, but we called him "Mr. Clean" because he always walked around like that toilet cleaner guy on TV—all smug with his head shaved bald and wearing a tight white T-shirt with the sleeves rolled up. And even though our team was pretty good, we could never get the best of that big dope's wily, smiley Coyotes.

My dad didn't like Cartridge either. First off, Cartridge always played the role of the big, butt-strutting policeman who never quite got around to removing his gunbelt before he arrived at the ballpark, so all the boys would be mightily impressed while he peacocked around with his pistol and shells.

Once, Mr. Clean gripped his gun, looked at my dad and said, "This here's my best friend, Pops. Never know when I might run into a few wetbacks," using the chicken-slang term people like him called the Mexicans who worked the crops in the nearby fields.

"What're you afraid of?" asked Dad. "Honest men doing an honest day's work?"

You see, Dad had a thing about honesty, and what bothered him most of all was *why* the Coyotes always won. Before the season started, Cartridge had contacted the best players he knew from the nearby leagues and told them to come over and "sandbag" their tryouts for our new Little League. That is, to make themselves look bad on purpose, so the rest of the coaches wouldn't know how good they really were and would pick other players instead.

"He sandbagged all of us," said Dad. "Suckered us in like Bozos, just so he could stack his team with talent and win a stupid trophy."

"He's the Bozo," Frankie says. "We're gonna win that

trophy, Mr. Ritter. I don't care who those guys are." He turns to me. "Right, Johnny? We're the Alley Cats and we're gonna win it for your dad."

"Abso-shootin'-lutely," I say, happy to agree, though I had no idea how we'd pull it off.

A few days later, before practice, Mr. Cleancut cruises by the high school, driving a brand-new metallic blue '63 Dodge Dart convertible. Straight off the showroom floor. That's the one with the push-button TorqueFlite transmission, V-6 engine, dual exhaust pipes, and bucket seats. "Like you're sitting in a movie theater, Pops," he tells my dad. "This baby'll go over a hundred and ten miles an hour and still get me twenty miles to the gallon." He pulls out a scrawny notepad and waves it at him. "I keep track of every tankful right here."

"I bet you do," says Dad, who's lugging a duffel bag full of gear and trying his best not to call the guy a bald-faced liar. See, back then, most cars—TorqueFlite tranny or not—averaged more like ten miles to the gallon, give or take five.

A few moments later, Frankie elbows me in the ribs. I look at him. He nods once, then taps his finger against his temple, signaling—secret agent style—that he had one great idea he'd love to tell me about, soon as we got off someplace where no spies could read our lips.

After practice, as everyone drifts off, Frankie walks up, backhands my shoulder, and says in code, "Meet me at *Barf*ridge's place at midnight tonight. Behind the garage. And we will guarantee our destiny and a place in history."

I don't question a thing. That's how we did it. "Mr. Bond," I respond, "I await our assemblagation with high expectations."

Near midnight, I show up at the old Cartridge ranch right on time. Frankie's already there, sitting in the backyard on a broken-down tractor, near the old barn. Next to him was a can of gas.

"You gonna burn the place down?" I whisper, my voice full of hope, dread, and expectation.

"No," he whispers back. "Not tonight. I got another idea. Follow me."

So I do, following behind Frankie as we slip through the unlocked garage doorway. He proceeds to the sleek new Dodge and twists off the gas cap.

"You gonna dump sugar in there?" I ask, knowing something like that would really gum up the works.

He shakes his head, saying nothing. He uncaps the red gas can and removes a short metal hose and tightens it onto the mouth of the can as a spout. He pours gas into the car's tank. Then he removes the spout, replaces the cap, and signals for us to leave. I follow him out, both of us hustling away from the ranch house.

Once we hit the roadway, I ask, "What was that for? Why are you *giving* him gasoline?"

He glances over. "My mom says I give everyone gas."

"No, I mean, really."

"Trust me," he says. "I got an idea."

So each night that week, Frankie and I sneak out and head to Cartridge's place, slink like alley cats into his garage, and pour some gas into the tank of his little pride and joy. Not a lot at first. Two quarts here, two quarts there. So he wouldn't notice. Then a gallon or so. Sometimes during a Coyotes practice, we'd sneak down the road and add a gallon, then add even more later that night. His gas mileage began to skyrocket. It became astronomical.

"Holy smokes, Pops," he tells my dad. "This little honey's getting forty miles to the gallon, now that she's all broke in. Forty miles per gallon!"

My dad had no desire to challenge him, though I was sure he thought Cartridge's figuring was finger-flicking stupid. But it was all the guy could talk about for the next two weeks. He just loved showing off. Frankie and I got him up to fifty-seven miles per gallon, before we finally let the air out of his tires, so to speak. For one week, we stopped adding any gas. After that, we started to siphon. A little each night. And then a little more.

And for the first time in recorded history, Mr. Gunsmoke grew noticeably quiet. Over the next several weeks, he even seemed rather depressed, you'd have to say, especially when the Coyotes started losing games. Cartridge had the car into the shop every other week replacing the fuel pump, fuel lines, spark plugs, the carburetor, and various other "likely suspects." Garret's dad was the mechanic, and he starts to suggest, "The guy's nuts. Sixty miles per gallon? Then forty, twenty, and now five?"

On the final night of our mission, Frankie did not bring along a gas can or a siphon hose. All he brought was a few packs of *saladitos*—dried plums, heavily salted—a family-sized bag of Cheetos—heavily cheesed—and a gallon-sized jug of his mom's fresh lemonade. "Tonight," he says, "we celebrate."

So we sat out on Cartridge's picnic table, under an old oak tree, eating Cheetos and saladitos, spitting out seed pits, licking our cheesy, salty palms, and washing it all down with big gulps of his mom's lemonade—the sweetest I'd ever tasted.

"Save your pits in a pile," he says. "We'll need them for later."

Once again, I question nothing. Part of the fun was to wait and see what Frankie had cooking. After we finished all the food and the lemonade, we just sat back and talked baseball a while, until finally, I couldn't stand it. My bladder was bursting. "Hey," I tell him. "I gotta go." I start eyeing the nearby bushes.

"Me, too," he whispers. He slaps my shoulder and signals me to follow him—inside the garage. "Come on. And let's bring all our trash too."

That's when I realized what he really had in mind.

Well, I won't say exactly what happened next, except

to accentuate the positive. Or, I should probably say, the *deposit*ive. That is, when we left for home a little while later—after our "pit" stops—that car had a lot more fuel in its tank than when we'd arrived. The quality, however, may have been somewhat diminished and highly acidic.

The Coyotes won the first half of the season, as had been expected, but Frankie continued to assert that we Alley Cats would win the second half, thus forcing those smugnuts into a playoff game for the league championship.

"I guarantee it," he told Mr. Hansen. "I'm working on a secret weapon," he told my dad.

Since we always talked like that, I didn't pay him much attention, but a few days later I did ask, "What secret weapon?"

"I'm studying all the baseball games on TV," says Frankie, "watching every single thing the pros do. Looking for clues." Then he elbows my elbow. "And I think I have the secret. I'll show you tonight at Lisa's."

Lisa Bjorn was Frankie's newest girlfriend, a tall sixth grader with long blond hair, dimples, and a ready supply of wide-eyed, hand-to-her-mouth laughs and giggles to anything Frankie said, no matter how stupid.

In other words, the perfect girl.

Lisa also had the largest, sweetest, and nicest-looking peaches you'd ever seen, growing from a massive tree in the middle of her backyard. Another definite plus.

I didn't mind going to her house either, since hanging around Lisa would mean a chance of seeing her friend Rita, a funny girl who I really liked, though no one knew it. Still, I was convinced, just by being in my presence, Rita would one day fall crazy mad in love with me.

So we get to Lisa's around eight, but instead of going up to the front door, Frankie leads me to a vacant lot behind her house. When I ask him why, he says, "At night, I prefer to enter the secret agent way."

Lisa's backyard fence was about six feet tall, with two-by-four braces on it running sideways. We step up onto a brace and hurdle ourselves over—like James Bond might do—and land in Lisa's yard.

He points to the peach tree, and says, "Let's climb up there. I got something to show you." Soon as we reach the tree, Frankie freezes and grabs my arm. "I just saw Lisa turn off the light in her room," he whispers. "She had her robe on. I think she's taking a bath."

"You wanted to show me that?" I ask. "What about the secret of baseball?"

He narrows his eyes. "One secret at a time."

We climb up and settle in, sitting on a couple of thick branches, and begin munching on peaches. "Keep an eye on Lisa's window," he says, pointing over his shoulder. "Tell me when the light comes back on. Things could get interesting."

We chow down on a couple of sweet, white-meat peaches each, but after a while, with nothing "interesting" to see, Frankie finally says, "Okay, listen. I got the secret of baseball right here." He takes a final mouthful of peach, chews a few times, and raises his eyebrows.

"What're you talking about? Lisa's peaches?"

"No, no, man." He finishes off the last of it, wipes his hands on his pants, then reaches back and pulls something mysterious out of his pocket. Slowly, between cupped hands, Frankie displays an unopened cellophane packet about the size of a deck of cards.

I read the wrapper. "Red Man Chewing Tobacco."

"This is what we've been missing," he says, and peels back the plastic. "It's the one secret ingredient you gotta have to play championship ball, like real Major Leaguers. They all chew this stuff."

He cracks the pack open, and immediately an odor I could only describe as "tobacco honey" fills my nose. We both consider it in wonder, and though I knew we were thinking the same thing, neither of us asked the most pressing question. *What exactly do you do with it?*

Frankie moves first. He snaps off a corner of the little brick, about the size of his thumb. "Here, watch me," he says. "Just stick it in your mouth, back against your cheek, and start chewing. It's chewing tobacco, right?"

Made sense to me, so I follow his lead and break off

an equal-sized bite of my own. Then I shove it back inside my cheek. And, *whoa*. I remember one time I stuck a spoonful of sinus-melting horseradish into my mouth at Thanksgiving—thinking it was some sort of fancy pudding in that little glass bowl and all. But this beat that mouth-fire all to pieces. Every spit gland I have spurts out at once. Even so, we just sit there and chew without saying anything.

A little spit dribbles down my throat. Big mistake. Man, I'd rather've drunk a long, tall bottle of hot sauce.

I squint at Frankie, who by then was leaning over the side of the tree with his eyes closed. "Boy," I say. "Strong stuff."

Frankie doesn't respond. Just hangs there. Then, with no warning, he pukes full-force, like a fireworks fountain, spewing peach chunk marmalade all over the ground. After three or four heaves, he finally says, "Don't swallow it, man. You're not supposed to swallow." And a big, long string of drool drips from his lips to the ground below.

That's when I happen to see the light in Lisa's bedroom flick on. "Hey," I say. "Look. She's back."

The next moment the heaves hit me. I fight to keep looking, to look up between barfs. But, no way. Last thing I remember before falling to the ground, is seeing Lisa standing at the window looking into the night, wearing a shiny blue robe, and pulling the curtain closed.

Every time we heard the pop and sputter of Mr. Clean's pretty little car come chugging down the street, Frankie and I would look at each other with a certain sense of satisfaction. And no one called it a Dodge *Dart* anymore, though the name everyone used did rhyme with "dart." But the best thing was that during the last half of the season, Frankie's prophecy came true. The new car that Mr. Swaggerpants could barely afford caused him such distraction that the Coyotes had fallen back to third place. And on the day the season ended, we Alley Cats had snuck up into first—right where we belonged—and into the first championship playoff game in the history of our league.

Frankie and I celebrated the occasion by jumping on top of the dugout and dancing. We actually were pretty good dancers, and when we spot Rita and Lisa walking down from the bleachers, Frankie decides to show them a grand finale. So he dances right off the edge of the dugout roof, lands on the ground, twists, spins, and twirls a few more times, then tumbles forward into a somersault calculated to end up on the ground in a splayed out position, with his feet at Lisa's feet, while grinning straight up at her smiling face.

And it worked perfectly.

Almost. The only hitch came when Frankie clopped his palms into the powdery dirt, so he could end his routine with "mystifying puffs of red dust," according to him. He got his dust. In fact, he was dust. Because he also just happened to slam his left arm into a mostly-buried boulder and cracked his wrist.

Before they took him to the emergency room, Frankie made sure to tell me, "Don't worry, man. I can still pitch. It's my other arm."

Suddenly, it felt like that sunken boulder had been lifted out of the ground and placed on my shoulders. I just looked at him, and said, "Oh yeah, sure, smart guy. Listen, this ain't bowling. In baseball, you pretty much need both arms."

Monday afternoon—playoff time—rolls around soon enough, and we all gather at the ballpark to warm up for the big game. Of course, Frankie is nowhere to be seen.

"Dad said the X-rays looked so bad," I tell everyone, "the doctor had to give Frankie pain pills. So he's probably still sleeping. He won't even get to play All-Stars."

Mr. Hansen announced that Darryl Flint, our backup pitcher who usually played third base, would pitch. That would give us a weaker infield on the left side, but no one said anything. We were too busy kicking stuff around the dugout, stealing glances at Martin Tubb, the cool Coyote fireballer, warming up down the sidelines. Every once in a while we'd mutter things like, "He's nothin'. Throws like Grandma Moses." And, "That rag arm won't last an inning."

We had almost run out of lies to tell each other when who should come around the corner and perch himself on the dugout steps, but Frankie Alvarez. His arm's in a full plaster cast stuck in a white sling hanging from his neck. And he's dressed in full uniform.

"Hey!" he screams. "Whatsa matta? Let's hear some *chat-ta!*"

He got to hear more than that. No one liked the fact that he had broken his arm by messing around right before this crucial game, and we let him know it. "What're *you* gonna do?" Nathan asked, without looking. "Keep score?"

Even Jeffrey climbed on. "You can't even coach the bases. You'd need your left arm to wave everybody around."

Our attitudes should've been better, but Frankie was our best pitcher and top RBI man. We needed his bat in the lineup and his butt on the mound.

Darryl Flint tried his best. He escaped the first inning, leaving the bases loaded. But in the second, they started off with two straight hits, then a walk to load the bases again. Not good. The next guy, though, smashes a line drive to me at short, which I manage to snag and quickly double up the runner in front of me, who had darted off second.

Just when it looks like we're going to get out of the inning with no damage, the next hitter drives in the first two runs with a single. After a walk and a hit batter, the bases re-load, and Darryl's on the verge of walking in another run when the next guy swings at a three-and-oh fastball, sending a hot shot up the middle. I dive for it, and snag it on pure luck, then flip it to second for the final out of the inning.

As we run into the dugout, none of us has any doubt that without a miracle, the Coyotes were going to cream us again.

We get no miracle. Instead, we get three quick at-bats and three quick outs. At least we were hitting the ball, I thought—nobody struck out—but the hits were not falling in.

As we grabbed our gloves to take the field, Frankie tells my dad something we can all hear. "Let me pitch," he says. "I can do it."

We freeze. If anyone else had suggested the idea, we would've all sneered. It was outside the realm of reality. Beyond belief. A guy on the mound with his arm in a sling? But the reality was, we were ready to believe in something better than the reality we faced. Dad was too.

If he could increase our chances—even to the tiniest degree—of beating Cartridge for the league championship, Dad would've listened to a drunken ump slumped against the dugout. So he tells Frankie, "Let's go to the mound and give you a little tryout."

Instead of warming up, the whole infield follows my dad, Frankie, and Mr. Hansen to the pitcher's mound.

We circle around and watch as Frankie plants his foot on the rubber, jiggles the ball in his bare hand, then sets two fingers on top of the red stitching—his fastball grip. He rocks back and starts his windup, raising his pitching hand about even with his ear, spins to the right a little, then steps forward and delivers a red-hot strike, knee high, right down the middle. His form was perfect.

My dad stares at the backstop a moment, then at Frankie. "How're you gonna catch the ball when Nathan throws it back?"

Frankie grins. "I got that all figured out. Nathan doesn't throw it to me, he whips it to Evan at first. And he'll be walking in to catch it, then flip it to me."

Mr. Hansen rubs his stubbly chin. "Well, I don't know." He turns to me. "Johnny, what about you pitching for us? Feel like giving it a try?"

"No, thanks," I say. What was this? Open tryouts in the middle of a championship game? "I'm too wild. Darryl's better than I am."

Every eyeball in the bunch turns toward my dad. He looks and looks at Frankie and finally just shakes his head, saying, "Forget it. Cartridge'll never go for it. He'll claim you're out of uniform or something for not wearing a glove."

And just then here comes Barfdish, scurrying up like a skunk to stick his big nose in and find out what's going on.

He looks at Frankie standing there with his white plaster cast and cotton sling and busts out grinning. "What's goin' on here, Hansen?" he says. "Alvarez can't pitch. He's a cripple."

Dad glares at him. "His pitching arm still works. And we're still thinking."

"That's right," says Mr. Hansen, raising his voice, standing right up to Carpfish. "We haven't decided yet. He's gonna throw a few more."

Frankie grins, big and bright. "Yow-za. I wanna throw a few more."

Evan lobs him the ball. Frankie winds again and lets fly with a rocket—five feet over Nathan's head.

"Wait, wait," he says. "I lost my balance. Give me another one." His next pitch bounces in front of home plate. He kicks his shoe into the dirt to adjust the toe hole on the mound. "I'm just a little off balance," he says, but then he flings a curveball three feet wide that Nathan has to dive for. "Oh, man," says Frankie.

We all groan. This, we realize, is not going to work.

Now Cartridge is smiling like a polecat in a fish pond.

My dad's face grows dark. Frankie straightens up and says, "It's okay, Mr. Ritter. I vow to you. I just gotta get my balance."

"Geez, Pops," says Cartridge. "Can't one of these other clowns pitch? You guys that desperate?"

That was one thing he should not've said to my dad.

My dad was never desperate. Ticked off, maybe. Ready to pop a polecat in the pucker, maybe. But not desperate.

Dad walks up and sticks his face about a foot away from Cartridge's and says, "Alvarez is pitching." He pauses. "That gonna bother you?"

Mr. Notbright pinches his big, fat lips into an ugly kiss, then shakes his head. "Nope," he says, "not a bit. It's your call, Geritol."

The umpire made Frankie wear a glove on his left hand, so he'd be in proper uniform. Well, actually, Mr. Hansen ran to his truck and brought back a roll of duct tape, and they *taped* the glove onto his hand, over the cast. Then Cartridge makes us use up two bottles of iodine painting the white sling orange, so it wouldn't camouflage the ball. But finally, Frankie's set and ready to go.

We hope.

I keep telling myself, "He can't be any worse than me." As if that was any consolation.

The umpire calls, "Play ball," and Frankie turns around and looks at all of us. He tosses the ball up and down in his bare hand. Then he yells, "Let's hear some *chatta*!" Mr. Hansen echoes the call from somewhere down inside the dugout. And we do. We chatta like it mattas.

The first pitch of the inning is perfect. Smack dead

center of the plate, fastball, knee high, just like his first warm-up toss. Nathan even holds the ball in his mitt a moment extra, just to savor the umpire's call. "Steee-rike one!"

Whatever balance he'd lost during his warm-ups, he must've regained in a hurry, because Frankie goes on to "steee-rike" out the whole side that inning. Three up, three down. And this time the Alley Cats *howl* all the way to the dugout. I mean, we go crazy.

In our half, Garrett leads off with a soft single. His little brother Evan sacrifice bunts him to second. Then I score him with a triple to right. I'm serious. Fastball. Inside corner. And I turn on it like the guy was flipping me a peach from a tree.

Normally Frankie would be up next, but he wasn't batting in his usual spot, so Nathan got the honor of blasting a single to left and knocking me in. And just like that, we're back in the game, 2–2.

In the bottom of the fourth, Frankie comes up to bat with one out and Jeffrey standing on second. Of course, we all know this is going to be ugly, because Frankie can't even hold the bat. He just stands up there with the stick on his right shoulder. Three straight strikes, and he's out, is what we figure.

But Frankie does not figure the way normal people do. Instead, he chokes way up on the handle, like he's holding a hatchet. And the first pitch he sees, he just yanks back and hacks at it, chopping a bouncer right through the middle and into center field. Base hit. Jeffrey scores. We're leading, 3–2!

On the next pitch—get this—Frankie steals second and even slides. No problem. But it gets better. The catcher airmails his throw into center, and when Frankie sees it, he bounces back up and starts "motorvatin'" along like Chuck Berry chasing Lucille in her Coupe de Ville. He's got third base in his hip pocket, when, right at shortstop—between second and third—he jams on the brakes and skids to a dead stop.

We're all on the dugout steps screaming, "Go, man! Go!" The fans behind us are going ape-o-leptic. "Run, run!" they shriek. "Don't stop!"

By then, the shortstop'd run down the ball and flung it to third, making an over-the-shoulder, off-balance toss which is on line, but not all that strong.

As soon as Frankie sees the ball, reads the arc and speed, he resumes motorvatin'. The ball bounces a few times on its way to the third baseman's glove. And Frankie bounces once himself, on his way to the third baseman's glove. What I mean is, Frankie had timed his slide so that his foot reached that glove just ahead of the baseball. And with a natural little slide-motion, secret-agentary kind of kick—one which no one could've rightfully accused him of inflicting for any other purpose than the simple employment of normal aggressive baserunning—he sends the ball flying back from whence it come. Then he bounces up again and trots on home for another run.

"What was that all about?" I asked. "You crazy?"

"What?" he says, plopping himself onto the bench. "I knew I had third in my pocket. But I didn't wanna get stuck out there. We needed the run. Who knows what you clowns would've done?"

While Frankie rested, all we clowns did was get hit after hit and run after run. By the time the game ended, we had not only piled up eight more runs to win the 1963 league championship 11–2, but not a single one of those Coyotes ever got another hit. Frankie had done the impossible. He had pitched four innings of no-hit, no-run ball with a broken arm.

But, wait—that wasn't the impossible part. What I loved was this. During his little third inning "tryout"—with everyone gathered around the mound watching him throw wild pitch after wild pitch—he had sand-bagged Cartridge into thinking he couldn't play worth beans. He'd suckered him in and took that trophy right out of his hands.

Later that night, Frankie and I are sitting in Cartridge's Dodge, with our feet on the dash, tugging on beef jerky, sucking on saladitos, and drinking long, tall bottles of RC Cola. And I realize, Francisco "Frankie" Alvarez was one of a kind. One of the finest eyeball-to-eyeball tall-tale tellers and outright jokesters I'd ever met, and definitely the type of guy you wanted to have on your side for the ride of your life. "And here the whole time," I tell Frankie, "I just thought you were crazy."

Frankie closes his eyes and spits out a plum seed. "I am," he says. "Same as you. Baseball crazy."

And we both knew, truer words will never be spoken.

INF ✦ Charles R. Smith Jr. ✦ 4

POSITION: UTILITY MAN | *ROOKIE YEAR: 1999

POSITIONS: author/poet/photographer

*BBI: 22

CAREER HIGHLIGHTS: Caught a number of Nolan Ryan fastballs in Texas while working on a photo shoot. Even though my right hand was taped up pretty good, it still hurt for days after that.

FAVORITE TEAM: New York Yankees

FAVORITE PLAYER: Reggie Jackson

BEST GAME EVER: First game in Yankee Stadium after I moved to New York in 1991.

JUST LIKE GRAMPY

by Charles R. Smith Jr.

So there I am on the mound sweatin', the sun pushing the mercury as high as it would go. But the sun
wasn't responsible for opening every pore in my body
and soaking my skin. No, my dripping brow and soaked
palm are courtesy of the batter standing at the plate;
the one home run I gave up earlier and another that
just missed by a few feet.

Coach comes out to tell me to watch my arm slot,
sayin' I'm releasin' too high.

"You lucky he fouled that one off. Step off the gas a
bit and work the curve," he says.

*Forget the curve. Give 'em the gas. Gas 'em out the
box!*

Who said that?

I turn around but there's no one there except a hot breeze.

I turn my attention back to the box and when my catcher drops two fingers, I crank a curve from behind my back that gets yanked foul to the right. Again.

Coach starts out onto the field but I wave him off.

I know what I'm doin'. I know what I gotta do and nobody's gonna help me do it. I just gotta do it.

Two balls, two strikes. Two—one us. One man on.

The winning run staring at me in the box with two outs.

I need one strike. Now.

Some things you inherit in life whether you want them or not, and much to the dismay of my two older brothers, I inherited my grampy's rocket of a pitching arm; strong and lefty.

It revealed itself in our backyard on my third birthday. The youngest of three by a good four years, I toddled through a game of catch when the baseball rolled in front of me. Dad asked me to throw it to him, so I did. Left-handed, straight and hard. The ball went flying and Dad's mouth flew open.

"Looks like Dad's arm landed smack dab on you, kiddo."

My grampy played in the big leagues years ago and if I could throw like him, then hey, maybe I could play in the big leagues too. He was so good, Dad said, that he had what they called "electric stuff." At three years old I didn't know what that meant but I knew that someday I too wanted to have "electric stuff." Just like Grampy.

Dad, me, my two brothers, and Grampy started tossing complete weekends away with the baseball once Grampy heard I inherited his big-league arm. Our weekend games between the five of us went on for a good couple of years, but as we all got older, it whittled down to just me and Grampy, my dad busier with work and my older brothers one day saying, "The old man's gone nuts" after giving me all their baseball gear.

"'At's it kiddo. Bring on the heat. Gimme the gas," he would shout every time the ball whipped from my hand to his mitt, and after so many summers of givin' Grampy the gas in the backyard, I had what he liked to call "a bona fide heater."

"I'm seein' more of me in you every day, and someday you'll have my e-lec-tric stuff too," he'd say with a wicked grin and shake of my shoulder.

I could sure use some e-lec-tricity right now.

I punch my mitt. Not once. Not twice. But three times. Each time harder than the last, and on the third punch a hot flame shoots up from my fingers, through my wrist, past my forearm, past my elbow, and into my shoulder, making my left arm hot.

I stare at it.

Looks fine. On the outside. But on the inside my muscles, veins, bones, marrow, and blood cells feel hotter by the second. My arm feels like it's on fire.

Everything in my body speeds up: my breathing, my thoughts, my heart, my hands.

Now we're cooking with gas. Come on, kiddo. Burn 'em out the box.

Kiddo?

Grampy?

I swivel my head around the park. Where'd that come from? Grampy's not here. First the heat is making me sweat, now it's frying my brain.

Shake it off. One more strike and this game is over.

I go into my motion and release. High. Too high. And fast. Too fast. Into-the-fence-behind-the-ump fast.

Three balls, two strikes.

Come on, kiddo. Focus!

I step off the rubber and my mind bolts from the batter in the box, back in time to the first time Grampy took me bowling. He suggested I give it a try to help with my pitching motion. And focus.

"Now kiddo, I know they aren't quite the same thing, but pitching and bowling involve a lot of motion mechanics, and if you can figger 'em out in bowling, then you can figger 'em out in pitching. Plus, it feels good smacking a buncha pins around."

The sound of pins being smacked and scattered shattered the silence the moment I stepped through the bowling alley door for the first time. Big guys, little guys, big women, little women, and everyone else in between laughed and slid and rolled and bowled on assorted lanes, the balls knocking into pins with all sorts of speed and spin. Bodies moved slow, fast, hesitant, confident, and clumsy. Some rolled the ball. Some hurled the ball. Some threw the ball. Some simply pushed the ball between their legs.

"I don't get it. Only a child would do that and she ain't no child," Grampy said, pointing his thumb toward a pear-shaped woman no older than my mom, in the lane next to us. She inched her way to the line on her tippy toes, held the ball between both hands, then swung the ball down between both legs before pushing it over the line with a big "ummmmph!" The ball inched its way down the lane as she inched her way backward and to the side, right into Grampy preparing to throw his ball.

"Ay, watch out there," Grampy said, irritated that his steps were thrown off. "You got your lane. I got mine. So stay in yours."

"Sorry," came the whispered response from the woman while her husband, sitting nearby, perked his ears and swiveled his head as Grampy got back into his stance: feet squeezed close together, back bent slightly, ball in his left hand with his right hand protecting it on the side, and short breaths puffing from his mouth like a bull in a ring. His eyes narrowed in on the pins like the same bull now seeing the red cape drop.

One step. Two steps. Slide. Release.

A smooth underhand motion sent the ball spinning down the lane the same way his smooth overhand motion sent his fastball spinning toward the plate. Two different motions, one result: a strike. Ten pins scattered as the ball crashed its way through each, splashing a big "X" onto our scoreboard.

"That's how you do it!" Grampy shouted, high-fiving me while eyeballing "the child" and her husband.

The husband huffed, then pushed himself up from his seat.

"'Scuse me there, Pops—"

"I ain't your pops," Grampy interrupted.

"Whatever—this is my wife's first time and I'd 'preciate it if you cut her a li'l slack. You know, with the trash talk and such," the husband said, holding his neon green ball in one hand while polishing it with a cloth in the other.

"Trash talk? Is that what you think I was doing?" Grampy laughed, slapping his hands onto his hips. "Heck, if I wanted to trash talk I'da said something a whole lot meaner 'an 'at," he added, scratching his head. "I mean, I'da said something like—"

"Grampy, come on—"

"I'da said something like . . . she ain't no child but she sure bowls like one, or . . . "

"What'd you say, old man?" the husband said, putting his ball down and stepping toward us.

"Come on, Grampy, let's go."

"Or if I really wanted to talk some trash I'da said something like, I dunno—some people got about as much grace as a bull in a china shop, or . . . "

"I've had just about enough of you. Anything else comes out of those gums a yours and I'm gonna hafta—"

"What? You gonna hafta what?" Grampy sneered, cocking his gray crew cut to the side.

"Come on, Grampy—"

"Naw, naw, kiddo. This gentleman here thinks your grandfather is talking—what'd he call it?—trash to his wife. But you know me, kiddo. If I really wanted to talk trash, I'da said something like"—Grampy looked from me to the husband—"some people need to stay on the couch where they belong."

"That's it, old man," the husband said, crossing from his lane onto ours.

I stepped in between the two and faced the oncoming husband, eyes blazing, lips sneering and all.

"Listen mister, we meant no disrespect. Really. My grandfather gets a little . . . "

"What, kiddo?" Grampy said, now eyeballing me. "I get a little what?"

"My grandfather here was just so excited to show me how to throw a strike that—he didn't mean what he said. It's just"—I glanced a good foot above me at the husband—"he gets fired up and—"

"Yeah well, one day he's gonna get burned," the hus-

173

band hissed before grabbing his ball and his wife to leave the alley.

Grampy flipped me around to face *his* blazing eyes, red face, perked ears, and frothing lips. We stood eye to eye.

"What's 'at all about, kiddo? I can fight my own battles. I *was* in a war, y'know. I don't need your help," he said, finger in my chest, nose to nose.

I took a step back, then smacked his arm the way he always did mine. "Forget them, Grampy. I wanna see another strike from this arm of yours."

"Ohhh, I got plenty of those left in me," he said, cooling off a bit before getting back into his stance, but this time he wasn't silent; his lips moved in a mumble, and the mumbles grew louder as he stepped toward the line.

"Pops . . . old man . . . *hmmph* . . . ain't nobody's old man . . . plenty left in *this here arm*!" he said, stepping quick toward the line before hurling a rocket down the slick lane and smashing the pins like a clap of thunder echoing across the alley, turning all eyes on us.

"See that, kiddo? You see what I just did?" he said, eyes wide. "That right there is the secret."

"Secret to what? What secret?"

He inched closer to me and looked me in my eyes before pointing to his.

"Strikes. It's all about focus. You gotta take all that fire in you and harness it," he said, squeezing his left fist. "Focus it and unleash it on your target." His clenched fist opened and shot out toward the pins. "Like a lightning bolt."

I stared at the pins, then back at him in silence.

"Once my fire got stoked by ol' hothead, I put it to work and *burned* them pins," he said, pointing down the alley before shouting, "*The old man still has the fire!*" He then spun around, pointed to me, and added, "And one day you will too, kiddo."

"But . . . I don't have any fire," I said.

He laughed. "That's funny, 'I don't have any fire.' Everybody's got fire, kiddo. It's just a matter of finding the match that sparks it."

Back at the house I thought about what Grampy said, about this whole fire thing, and told Grammy. She was the ice to Grampy's heat and reminded us that that was just how he played the game; with plenty of passion and fire. It served him well on the field, she said; unfortunately, off the field he never learned how to "control his fire." I still remember the way those last few words came out of her mouth, with a whisper and a soft head shake, letting me know that like me and my brothers, she'd somehow been singed by his flame as well.

I blink myself back into the present, punch my mitt, and take deep breaths to relax but can't. My arm is getting hotter by the second and for the first time I'm getting introduced to *my* fire. Each breath pumps oxygen into the flames in my arm and each flame leaps from my arm into my chest into my heart and spreads through my body, down to the toes on my feet, up to the flaming red curls on my head.

The batter in the box turns into Grampy in the bowling alley, standing in his bowling shoes, staring at me with eyes blazing.

You gonna use that fire or what, kiddo?

The heat doesn't feel good, but the more I try to fight it, the hotter it gets. The hotter it gets, the hotter I get. At Grampy. And his cursed arm. And his cursed *fire*. Too many times I saw that fire unleashed, particularly when it came to any kind of competition, especially baseball; an umpire calling out one of his beloved Dodgers on TV; my oldest brother hitting "just" a single instead of a double; my second-oldest brother dropping a ball; or me walking somebody. That was the worst—me walking somebody. Every team I pitched on, I was the best by a country mile but if I wasn't throwing strikes, well . . . I just wasn't doing Grampy's arm justice. And he'd let me know it. His soft smile hardened. His droopy ears perked up. His once pale skin turned tomato red by the second. And those eyes; they went from cool blue to hot red in a blink. He was silent during this transformation and the fuse didn't ignite the gunpowder until those first words came out: *"Ohhhh, come on . . . "* But when they entered the world surrounded by a storm of spit, that's when he went off.

My grandfather was no longer sweet old Grampy, but a bomb exploding before my eyes. Foam frothed at his mouth and words flew so fast from his lips that it was hard to understand what he was saying. Anybody sitting near him at a game would scatter like bugs when the lights go on.

Come on, kiddo, focus. No walks!

I step off the rubber and smack my mitt. Hard.

Full count.

I don't want Grampy's fire. I don't want my neck muscles to bulge. I don't want my ears to perk up. I don't want to turn the color of a tomato. I don't want to yell at ball games on TV. I don't want my grandkids holding me back from fistfights. I don't want to scare my grandkids to the point they don't want to play any games with me, especially baseball. I don't want to . . . I don't wanna die of a heart attack in the bleachers because my grandson gives up a homer. Just like Grampy. Just last month.

I just want this game to be over.

Gas 'em out the box!

I tug on my cap and put the fire to work. I focus in on the mitt, harness the heat, and unleash a lightning bolt right down the pipe.

Strike three.

The smack of leather echoes across the field like a clap of thunder.

Just like Grampy.

POSITION: LEFT FIELD | *ROOKIE YEAR: 1971

*BBI: Thus far, I've had over 120 books published. (But lots of them were short ones. Mere bunts, if you will.)

CAREER HIGHLIGHTS: I have to admit that I don't think in terms of highlights when it comes to my own life. I'm just enjoying it altogether too much. My first story in *National Geographic*? Being on a panel at ABA in Miami with Oprah Winfrey? Winning the Lifetime Achievement Award from the Native Writers' Circle of the Americas? Or just still being able to get up in the morning, sit down in front of my computer, and have the words come to me . . .

FAVORITE TEAM: Hate me if you must, but it's the Yankees. (When they were in Brooklyn, though, it was the Dodgers.)

FAVORITE PLAYER: The one and only "The Mick," Mickey Mantle. I can still hear the song that was written for him—"I Love Mickey!" (And then Mantle himself says "Mickey who?" and is answered "Mickey YOU!")

BEST GAME EVER: It was 1961, the last game of a regular season that had been spectacular as Mickey Mantle and Roger Maris both chased Babe Ruth's magical record of 60 home runs. But Mickey had gotten no further than 54 and Roger had stalled at 60 on September 26. On that October 1, against the Boston Red Sox, Maris came up to bat and clobbered the ball for number 61 in a game that ended with the Yankees winning 1–0.

*Stat key: BBI=Books Batted In (number of books published)
Rookie Year: first book published

BALL HAWK

by Joseph Bruchac

"Indians invented baseball."

That's what Uncle Tommy Fox said on the day I was ready to throw in my glove and quit the Long Pond High School team for good. It was one of his typically cryptic remarks and, as usual, it started me thinking.

Quite frankly, if Uncle Tommy hadn't come into my life when he did, I probably would have ended up dyeing my hair purple and going goth. (I would, I might add, have been the first to do that in Long Pond High School, which is barely big enough to have cliques. My high school's size is one of the reasons why I was still, pathetic as I was with a glove and a bat, a regular member of the varsity nine. There just weren't that many eligible candidates.)

Uncle Tommy, though, saved me from turning my back on being a skin. I'd been hanging around Uncle Tommy ever since he moved up here to work in the Indian Village and my mom introduced him to me in her German accent.

"Mitchell, it vould be gut for you to meet anudder real Indianishe mann und he vas ein freund of you vater."

It wasn't just that Uncle Tommy was, indeed, a real Indian, albeit of a different tribe than my father. Or that this broad-shouldered old Indian guy with long gray braids and a friendly face really did seem to like me and enjoy taking on that role of being an uncle. Or that he knew more about being Indian, really being Indian, than anyone else I'd ever met. He also had a sense of humor and we both needed it when it came to me and baseball. For some reason, everyone thought I should be playing it. True, I'd always been good at other sports like football and wrestling, but baseball had me buffaloed. My mother had gotten it into her head that being an Indian I should of course not just play baseball but excel at it. Even striking out in nineteen consecutive at-bats had failed to disabuse her of that certainty.

Why baseball? Well, as little as my mom knew about American sports, she had heard of the Cleveland Indians and the Atlanta Braves. So she figured it was a game that honored Indians and thus I should be part of it. Yeah, I know. But try to explain to an eager German immigrant mother about stereotyping and American Indians being used as mascots.

Plus my dad had been a really great baseball player. He'd been playing armed forces ball when Mom met him in Germany.

He was the best baseball player in the history of our family. He was even better than his grandfather, who'd played baseball at the Carlisle Indian School and in the summer Carolina semi-pro leagues with Jim Thorpe. On the ball field, my Dad was unstoppable. He could hit almost any pitch. If he'd had the right breaks, and hadn't gotten his right knee ruined when he was in the service, he could have gone pro.

We played pitch and catch together almost every day during the seven years we shared before his truck was hit head-on by a drunk driver, leaving his half-Indian son to be raised in the sticks by the wife he had brought back with him at the end of his tour of duty with the marines, which had concluded in der Vaterland.

Anyhow, going back to that day when I was ready to pack it all in, it was a game we were sure to win. But even though we were leading the Hurleytown Hornets by a score of 6–0 and it was the bottom of the seventh inning, I still had to take at least one more turn at bat. When there's only twelve guys on your whole team and you're the center fielder, you can't avoid it.

I wiped my hands on my knees, knocked imaginary dirt off my cleats. Nineteen, I thought.

The Hurleytown pitcher smiled when he saw me come up to the plate. All the pitchers in the Northern league did that. Then he mouthed the words. Easy out. I hate it when they do that.

I looked over toward the stands. My mom was smiling and nodding at me, even though she had both fists clenched around her soda can so hard that it looked like an hourglass. Uncle Tommy, who was next to her, just kept his face blank. I was grateful for that.

The pitcher wound up, kicked high just to show off, and let it go. Fastball, high and outside just where I like it. I took a cut that would have knocked down a wall if I'd been holding a sledgehammer. Unfortunately all I had was a bat. WHIFFF!

Strike one.

I don't have to tell you what happened with the next two pitches. Just the usual. Twenty in a row.

Mercifully, we finished the game without my coming around in the batting order again and us winning 7–1. I took my time in the locker room, soaped my long black hair and rinsed it out twice. Half of me hoped everybody would be gone by the time I came out. But the other half of me desperately wanted to not be alone, wanted somebody to be there waiting for me.

That's what I was thinking as I shuffled out of the gym, my duffel bag in one hand and my towel in the other. Then I saw Uncle Tommy still sitting there, all alone in the bleachers. He raised a hand, gesturing for me to join him.

It might have been my mom who encouraged Uncle Tommy to stay around and wait for me. But maybe not. After all, Uncle Tommy had been faithfully watching in the stands each time I whiffed out. He came to all my games, not just football in the fall, where I'd found my groove in my sophomore year at both tight and D-end. Tackling other ballplayers, blocking and snagging the occasional pass were right up my alley. Unlike trying to tag that white little pill with either glove or bat.

"Indians invented baseball," Uncle Tommy said again. We were sitting at the very top of the stands where we had a great view of the high peaks that were beginning to turn red in the setting April sun. I knew he had to get back to his place and check on the hawks before dark, but he wasn't making a move to stand up, so I stayed put. My uniform was in my bag, but I had pulled my glove out and I was punching my left fist into it.

I looked up at him, ready to smile if I saw him grinning. But his face was serious.

"You know what I mean," he said.

Well, I did. I'd heard the whole rap before. There were no team sports in Europe before those early explorers stumbled into the new world and found Indians playing all kinds of team games—from lacrosse to basketball. Rubber balls were invented by Indians.

But I didn't say anything. I just pounded my glove a little harder.

Uncle Tommy looked up and nodded his head. I followed his gaze. There was a distant speck getting closer. A very big bird, the circle of its soaring flight carrying it closer to us. It wasn't Hawk or any of the other birds that Uncle Tommy was nursing back to health. It was bigger. An eagle. Pretty soon it was right overhead. I wondered how Uncle Tommy could do that. Call a great bird like that to us.

Folks around here knew that whenever anyone came across a big bird that had been hurt, maybe tangled with a power line or sideswiped by a truck, a hawk or an owl or even an eagle like the one above us, they could bring it to Uncle Tommy. He didn't have one of those federal licenses to care for birds of prey, but whenever game wardens came out to check on him, they never found anything. Uncle Tommy never caged or tied down any of his birds. He let them fly free. If they were too hurt to fly he kept them somewhere safe that the federal people couldn't find.

Sometimes Uncle Tommy made it all seem so easy.

"Mitchell," he said, "things that are supposed to come easy aren't always that easy to do."

Uncle Tommy, the mind-reading Zen master.

"Meaning what?" I said, like I was supposed to do.

"Do you like playing baseball?" Uncle Tommy asked. Of course he was not answering my question.

"Baseball is great," I said. "It's just me. I stink."

"Hmm," Uncle Tommy said. Not a question, not a comment, but a lot more than both.

"Okay, so I'm good at running bases. Better than most, I guess. And when I do finally get the ball I can throw it hard and straight. But half the time I go out to shag a fly ball, I miss it. You ever notice how when I yell 'I've got it,' all the other fielders start praying?"

"Hmm," Uncle Tommy said again. He really wasn't going to let go of this, was he?

"Well, what about my batting?" I asked. "The only way I could ever get a hit was if the ball was as big as a watermelon and you set it up on a tee."

"And painted a bull's-eye on it?" Uncle Tommy said.

I couldn't help it. I had to laugh. For a while. Then I stopped, feeling empty inside.

"I quit!" I yelled, standing up and throwing my glove out onto the field. "I'm done with it."

Uncle Tommy didn't bat an eye at my temper tantrum. He just kept looking out at the mountains. So I stood there, not sure whether I should climb out of the stands and stomp off or go down on the field and pick up my glove.

"Why'd you say that?" Uncle Tommy finally asked in a soft voice.

"I hate this game!"

Uncle Tommy shook his head. "Why did you keep playing it so long?"

"Because the other guys won't let me quit. No... because my mom wants so bad for me to play base-ball."

"And why is that?"

"Because she's got some idea that Indians should play baseball."

"Why?"

"Because there are teams with Indian names. Right?"

I looked over at Uncle Tommy and he shook his head.

"Mitchell," he said, "I knew your dad when he played ball at Haskell Indian School. My playing days were way behind me then, but I was there teaching in the crafts program. He was good enough to have pro scouts looking at him until he decided to go with the military instead. But even then he was a star on those armed forces teams."

I started crying then. Uncle Tommy was right. My mom wanted me to play baseball because she knew how much Dad loved the game. She'd met him when she came to one of his games on the base in Germany. She fell in love with the way he ran like a deer after hitting the ball over the fence. Then she fell in love with him.

But he'd never be here in the bleachers to watch me play the game he loved best of all. I wanted so badly to connect with him that—even though I knew it was impossible—my mind was twisted against itself whenever I went out onto the field.

Uncle Tommy's hand was on my shoulder. He stayed silent until I'd cried myself out. Then he climbed down out of the stands with me when I went to pick up my glove—which had landed far out in left field.

"Time to check on the hawks," he said.

Uncle Tommy never drove. Instead he'd let me take him places in the old beater truck I'd bought with the money I'd earned working summers with him at the Indian Village, teaching the tourists about real Native people. Neither one of us said anything until we were almost at his place.

"Mitchell, maybe your mind is getting clear now, but you still need to train your eye," he said as we pulled in the drive. "We'll start tomorrow morning."

I came back at dawn. Of course he was already up and waiting for me with his own glove, a beautiful old Louisville Slugger, and a whole box of baseballs. All stuff that he'd stored in that little attic of his, which somehow seemed to have more storage space than a cargo ship. He'd never let me go up there, but he was always producing unexpected things from it. Like that time he brought down two saddles and blankets and all the gear for riding and roping calves. But that's another story.

"Batting practice," he said, pointing at the home plate he had set up against the side of his house.

Uncle Tommy had been a pitcher when he was in Indian school and it turned out he could still bring it—fastball, slider, even a tricky little curve.

"Focus," he'd say. "Don't see anything except that ball getting bigger. Connect." Then he would whiz another one past me. But by Sunday afternoon I started making contact.

"Are you slowing the pitches down?" I said.

"Nope." Uncle Tommy smiled. "You are." He got ready to throw again. "Relax with power," he said. "Hard and easy."

He had another trick up his sleeve. "The way we always used to learn," he said, "was by watching nature. I got another teacher for you here."

He wrapped a deerskin around his arm and we walked out back.

"Hawk," he called, holding up his arm. Uncle Tommy never gave names to wild animals more than that. A deer was just "Deer," a bear was just "Bear." But when he called out the word "Hawk," the one hawk he was calling to was always the one that would come. This time it was the big red-tail. It dove down out of the tree, braked with its wings, and reached out its big talons to grasp his arm.

"How can this hawk catch a bird in flight at ninety miles an hour?" Uncle Tommy said.

"Because he sees it?" I asked.

Uncle Tommy shook his head. He wanted me to think.

"Because he sees where it's going to be," I said.

"Go ahead," Uncle Tommy said. He lifted his arm and the hawk took flight. It whistled as it rose and then began circling overhead. I cut a piece of meat from the flank of the road-killed doe we'd picked up from the main road that morning. It was a piece about the size of a baseball. I cocked my left arm and heaved it.

Before it could hit the ground, that red-tail caught it out of midair with its claws.

Our next game was Wednesday afternoon. Instead of the usual heavy feeling of hopeless despair, I was feeling sick to my stomach. I felt like I might even throw up. And that wasn't a bad thing. Whenever I threw up in the locker room before I went out on the mat to wrestle, I usually ended up doing good. In another couple of minutes we'd be heading out on the field. My gut roiled.

"Excuse me, guys," I said, heading for the john.

"Hey," Robby Mills, our shortstop said, "Sabattis is about to lose his lunch."

"Cool," Zach Branch said. He was on the wrestling team with me.

It wasn't that big a game that day for most of us. It was the Carrier Falls Cougars we were playing and we'd beaten them already a few weeks ago by a score of 4–1, despite my striking out three times. But it was big enough for me. It started in the top of the third inning when I called for a fly ball and not only caught it, but threw it back in quick and hard enough to catch the Cougars runner who'd been on base between second and third. My first double play! Robbie almost cracked my ribs when he came running out from shortstop to hug me.

Bottom of the third, I was the second batter up. I looked up just before the pitch and thought I saw a bird circling above the field. Then the pitcher reared back and let it fly. It was a curveball. I saw that clearly as it came toward me. I swear I could even see that there was a smudge of green from the turf on the ball's lacing as it rotated toward me. My swing was strong, but relaxed at the same time. Hard and easy. And I connected.

The ball hit the sweet spot on the bat. It was a sound half crack and half chunk, a sound I had heard before, just plain music. And the ball was rising, heading up and out, and I knew it was going far past any of the fielders, way out beyond the fence. People were yelling at me to run, but I was just standing there, watching it go, flying toward the sun.

And that was when the yelling stopped. It stopped as that hawk dove. It caught the ball in its claws, banked, flapped its wings, and floated off toward the distant mountains, taking what should have been my first home run with it.

"You got it, Dad," I whispered. Don't ask me why I said that or if it makes any sense. I mean, I knew it was just Uncle Tommy's red-tail.

I turned to the umpire, whose mouth was open as he watched the big bird disappear.

"Hey," I said in a soft voice, "I think I know what you should call it." Then I told him.

A big grin came to his face and he pointed off in the direction the hawk had gone.

He yelled it out and everybody in the park went wild.

The pitcher was so rattled by what had happened that he threw me an easy one on his next pitch that I stroked over the third baseman's head for a double.

I ended up that day with two more doubles and a sacrifice bunt to my credit. We won 5–2. And I played out the rest of that season with a batting average of .285 and a reputation as a better than average fielder. I even had a grand slam home run the last game of the season. But the best moment I ever had in baseball came that day against the Cougars. It came to me because of what Uncle Tommy taught me about letting go of anger and putting my heart in the game. It allowed me to have my best hit ever, even if it ended up being a foul ball.